I0691014

small stations fiction

Manuel Rivas

The Potato Eaters

Published in 2016 by
SMALL STATIONS PRESS
20 Dimitar Manov Street, 1408 Sofia, Bulgaria
You can order books and contact the publisher at
www.smallstations.com

Text © Manuel Rivas Barrós, 2016
English translation © Jonathan Dunne, 2016
Design © Yana Levieva, 2016
© Small Stations Press, 2016

This book was first published in the Galician language as *Os comedores de patacas*
by Edicións Xerais de Galicia (Vigo, 1991). This translation follows the tenth (2008)
edition. A list of our fiction titles can be found at www.smallstations.com/fiction.

The quotation on page 7 is from Vincent van Gogh, *The Letters of Vincent van
Gogh*, selected and edited by Ronald de Leeuw, translated by Arnold Pomerans
(Penguin Books, 1997).

*This work received a grant from the General Secretariat of Culture of the Ministry
of Culture, Education and University Planning of the Xunta de Galicia in the call
for translation grants of the year 2015.*

*Esta obra recibiu unha axuda da Secretaría Xeral de Cultura da Consellería
de Cultura, Educación e Ordenación Universitaria da Xunta de Galicia na
convocatoria de axudas para a tradución do ano 2015.*

ISBN 978-954-384-052-6

Manuel Rivas

The
Potato
Eaters

Translated from Galician by **Jonathan Dunne**

Small Stations Press

For Isa, who didn't want the devil to appear,
and for Martiño and Sol, great potato eaters

As for the Potato Eaters – it is a painting that will do well in gold – of that I am certain.

Vincent van Gogh to Theo van Gogh, *c.* 30 April 1885

My Mother

There is my mother, so thin and sad. Whenever I see her looking like that, with those eyes of a wounded animal, I feel like bursting into tears. She really loves me.

'You're a wretch,' she mutters. 'A complete disaster.'

I so want her to give me a kiss and to ruffle my blond, curly locks, the way they do to children at their First Communion before they've spilt something on top of their sailor's suit. I love her too.

'Go to hell, mother,' I say in such a loud voice it sends a shock of pain down my leg. 'I don't know why you had to come.'

My leg. What on earth is going on in there? I feel as if it's being gnawed by a mouse. The doctor told me everything would be fine, but one leg would be shorter than the other because the big bone, whatever it's called, the one that goes from here to here, splintered like the branch of a tree.

'I'm going to have a limp,' I tell my mother with a smile.

'Wretch!' she replies.

Luou, Spiderman, is in a really bad way. He's covered in plaster from head to toe, with just his face open, like a mummy. He went tumbling down the hill like a rag doll and got stuck on some iron railings. He makes for a pitiable sight. He'll spend months gazing up at the ceiling.

'He was the one driving,' I tell my mother. And I light a cigarette.

'Don't smoke in here, you wretch!'

We went to the airport to see the blue lights and to take Something and then to descend the Alvedro curves at 120. The car rose into the air as if it wanted to fly, and then it really did fly, gliding over the hillside until it landed at the bottom like a sluggish, spent duck. After the fall, we heard again the tape's Gypsy music, all alone in the world. We were in a garden. I can recall the scent, as of soapy water. Nothing was happening, the stars were in their places, luminous backstitches on the great vault. I fell asleep, licking the sweet blood of my lips.

'Put that cigarette out, you wretch!'

My mother really loves me. She feels for me.

'Why don't you just leave me alone?'

I hate seeing her like this.

Luou

Luou doesn't have a mother or anything. He's an outcast. I think he ran away from the reformatory a hundred times. What he likes best are cars. He knows everything there is to know about cars. Had he been driving, I have no doubt we would have coasted down the Alvedro curves. I wasn't fully convinced, but I said to him, 'Let me have a go, Luou.' 'Are you sure?' 'You'll soon see, Luou.' What can I say? No comment.

He was happy in the reformatory because the food was good and there was a video. But it was very close to the Avenue, and the hum of mechanics didn't let him sleep. He would jump over the wall, head into town and grab himself a good one. He would spend the night dodging sirens, doing handbrake turns, testing all the other wretches on their way to work at that hour of the morning, who held back in amazement. One of History's unsolved mysteries is how Luou had it in him to reach the pedals and look through the windscreen at one and the same time. When he got tired, he would head to the Main Breakwater, switch on the radio and smoke, hunched in the seat, his feet on the steering wheel. Luou told me that squid fishermen would shine their torches on him, but normally it was the police. One day, however, the police took him back to the reformatory, and he got turned away.

'What do you mean, you don't want him?' asked one of the officers from the patrol car, annoyed as if he'd just been told his son was not going to be accepted into a fee-paying school.

'He was born on the 24th of the 10th, 1974. Here are his papers. Check it out for yourself. Today's his birthday. He's now too old.'

'So what am I supposed to do with him?'

'That's your business,' replied the janitor coldly, hanging on to the door handle.

'Does he have any family?'

'It doesn't say.'

'Anyone who can take charge of him?'

'It doesn't say.'

'Come on, lad. You heard the man. They don't want you in here.'

The officer placed a hand on Luou's shoulder, opened

the door of the patrol car and indicated to him to get in. He was visibly moved.

'Damn it, lad. Someone had to give you a good spanking when you were young.'

'What happens now?' asked the colleague who was driving.

'They don't want the snotty-nosed kid in there. He's old enough to go to the clink.'

He was really overwhelmed. Luou told me that officer was one of the few people who cared for him during his life.

'It's a shame no one ever gave you a really good kick in the balls,' he said with moist eyes.

They took him back to the judge, a man with swollen eyelids who stank of alcohol. He had hair growing like shadowy grass in his nostrils and earholes. Outside, it was pouring down, the water washing away the city's stain-encrusted carpet. Luou looked at the female figures dressed in tunics, etched on the glass. They were reminiscent of men. There was also a marble statue showing its breasts, but devoid of any warm feeling. Everybody came and went with grim expressions, as if the woman with bare breasts did not exist.

The lawyer on duty, possibly influenced by the delinquent's size, took the case seriously and banged his fist on the desk. The judge muttered to himself, went 'hum, hum', and the lawyer apologized. Finally, Luou was allowed to go to prison and had a family for a while.

As for me, I don't think I'll talk about my studies and things like that. What I do have is a family.

Help

I have asked my mother to bring me the *Sentimental Recordings*. Ever since this all happened, I haven't known whether I'm sad or happy, calm or anxious, laughing in sorrow or weeping for joy. Sometimes my leg hurts, and that comforts me; other times, I can't feel it and I start trembling with cold, as if the bed's iron bars were lumps of ice and the plaster an icicle hanging from the ceiling. I have the TV remote, but I need Help. I've been a week now without listening to Help, without talking to Help. If only I could call Help, everything would be easier.

'Help! Hi, Help!'

'How's it going, boy?'

'OK. I have a broken leg, Help.'

'Ah, the King of Crutches!'

'It's 345 here.'

It's incredible. You give him your fan-club number, and he identifies you straight away.

'Dance then, Samuel! *Today, living.*'

Help is my favourite music presenter. His programme is called *Sweet Dreams*. Have you never heard it? It's really something very special. His voice has an echo. I'm not sure how to explain it. The world is full of preachers, but only Help knows the kind of key you need.

'You're on the edge of the abyss, aren't you? Take courage. One foot forward. *Today, unease.*'

Sweet Dreams always starts with a slogan that is a kind of feeling. For example, Help says, '*Today, awful,*' or '*Today, enjoyment,*' or '*Today, laziness.*' You find out lots of words you didn't know before or that didn't speak to you. Help always has a very specific term to hand to express your state of mind.

'How are you feeling today?' asks Help. And then he adds, for example, '*Today, hate.*'

The incredible thing is how Help manages to transmit the same feeling with his choice of music. If Help says, '*Today, happiness,*' then life that day is like paradise, old people giving crumbs to the pigeons in St Margaret's Park and all the faces in the galleries on the seafront imbued with sunlight. When Help says, '*Today, melancholy,*' my eyes mist over, and I let myself be led like a drop of rain sliding down the window of the Dársena café on an autumn evening. If you write down the slogans of a month and send them to the radio station, Help sends what he calls a *Sentimental Recording*. You can't imagine how well-behaved I can be when I want something. I managed to put together an *Anthology of Feelings*, the equivalent of eight *Sentimental Recordings*, each of which contains eight *Feelings*. Help is great at explaining. Our head is like a computer; a *Feeling* is a bit, an electric impulse; eight bits make a byte, which is to say a *Sentimental Recording*. With a byte, I can get my head in order for a week. With an *Anthology*, I can get by for a whole season – one spring, for example. Contrary to what you might think, it's not always a question of listening to optimistic recordings. In time, I have come to appreciate and even desire other states of mind. One of my favourites is '*Today, loneliness*'.

The doctor said in two weeks I should be able to walk

down the corridor on crutches and reach the public phone booth in Orthopaedics. I shall say, 'Hello, Help, it's me, 345!' And he will reply in his dinosaur's voice, 'Samuel, my friend, how is life?'

The Old Man

The only other patient is an old man. I shout at him because he's a bit deaf. Or he pretends to be. Because he hears things no one else can hear.

'The barn owl,' said the old man this morning as soon as he woke up.

'The what?' I shouted. It was as if we were talking to each other across a river and Luou was in the middle, in a floating coffin.

'The barn owl,' shouted the old man. 'It sang last night. Poor animal!'

This deaf old man is always hearing things. One night, I was woken up by a strange, metallic squeaking in the room. I'm not at all keen on things that make noise and don't let themselves be seen, like that mouse that keeps gnawing away at my leg. Whatever it was, it advanced across the floor, tick-tock, like an armour-plated clock. I held my breath. All I could hear was That Thing, very close, with its implacable footsteps, and in the distance, like the mooing of a cow, ships' sirens gently pulling on the mist. I sat up, leaning on my elbows, and coughed nervously to see what would happen.

'It's just a cockroach,' said the old man.

'You what?' I shouted, relieved by his bronchitic words, as if a buffalo hunter had come to my rescue.

'A cockroach. It comes and goes. Poor animal!'

The old man always says this, 'poor animal', as if every repulsive, interfering bug were an innocent, helpless soul in enemy territory. After all, this is supposed to be a hospital, not a shelter for cockroaches! That is what I shall say to Miss Cowbutt when she turns up in the morning, wrapped in her white gown, and starts sniffing around for tobacco as if she were inspecting a prison cell or a pigsty. Stop worrying about the smell and get that blasted animal out of here! That is what I shall tell her.

'Are you not asleep?' I asked the old man.

'On and off.'

'Right.'

'You know something, boy? I don't trust them. You can't go closing your eyes at my age. These nights are not for me.'

Now he was the one coughing. It was a deep-seated, spongy cough, as if he had lichen in there or something.

'Are you not cold, boy?'

To tell the truth, it was stifling in the room. A kind of dry heat that whitewashed your lips and throat.

'Stoke the fire, boy, and throw on a good log. Don't let the fire go out, boy. A house that doesn't have smoke coming out of its chimney is no use.'

This happens to him sometimes at night. To begin with, I thought he'd lost his mind and was about to ring for Miss Cowbutt or someone. But then I thought this would be no fun for the poor old man and let him carry on with his delirium. He calls to me and sends me on errands.

'Have you been to the mill, boy?' says the old man.

'Yes, sir,' I shout.

'Did you bring the bran?'

'I sure did.'

'The hell you did!'

The old man is in hospital for the same reason as me. He has broken a leg. Only he broke his when he fell out of a fig tree. From time to time, a daughter comes to see him, lugging lots of plastic bags and with a gold tooth that looks awful. It's not a pleasant visit, and I have the impression the old man is sorry he doesn't have a stick to hand with which to shoo her away. He always asks after the dog.

'The dog! The dog! Would you believe it...?'

She starts shouting so everybody can hear her. Patients from Orthopaedics who are still able to stand on their own two feet poke their heads out from nearby doorways.

'Would you believe it? His daughter comes to see him, God knows the sacrifice this involves, and all he can do is ask about the dog. Not about the children, the grandchildren or the work at home. No. About the lazy, good-for-nothing dog which doesn't even know how to bark properly!'

She crosses herself and goes red in the face, glancing around, as if someone else were doing the shouting.

'And how are you feeling today, pops?' she asks in a low, tender voice.

'Not well,' grunts the old man.

The daughter is quiet for a moment. She rummages around inside her bags. She glances from side to side, then behind and in front. She looks, but doesn't look, with froggy eyes.

'Not well! Not well, he says. Would you believe it? Seventy years old, and he decides to go searching for figs. What was he doing in the fig tree when he had everything he needed? Like a little child. Seventy years old, and climbing a fig tree like a little child. He even pees in his trousers, needs a helping hand, but he has to go and climb the fig tree.'

'Enough of that, woman, put a hundred pesetas in the slot,' says the old man.

'In the what?' asks the daughter in a different tone.

'In the television. It works with pesetas.'

'Well, I'll be damned! What will they think of next?' mutters the daughter as she rummages in her purse.

At night, the old man calls to ask if I have spread litter in the cowshed and shut the gates. The old man always makes me feel useful.

'And did you give the dog something to eat?'

'I sure did.'

'What did you give him?'

'A bone.'

'A bone. The hell you did!'

Miss Cowbutt

If my mother doesn't bring me the *Sentimental Recordings* soon, I'll go mad. The old man keeps on hearing animals. Neighing horses, snuffling pigs, his dog that howls, tied to the leg of the granary. There are also crows that, according to him, keep moving between Orthopaedics and Cardiology, flocks cawing from east to west. He seems concerned. He doesn't complain about it, but I have the impression there's something strange going on inside his leg. He's been given a bag to pee in and, whenever the desire overtakes him, he lets me know, as if he were going to some corner to do it on the ferns and brambles.

'I'm going to see if I can do a pee,' he declares solemnly. And then he turns his back on me.

I think the reason he does this is so I shall switch off the television and he can do it in silence. Sometimes he repeats the same thing until I've finally understood. It's one of those televisions that takes coins. You have to put in a new coin each hour. I have the remote, I jump between channels but, when the time is up, there's nothing you can do. It always cuts off at the best bit. So then I have to use the call button to summon Miss Cowbutt, who enters the field of fray, muttering under her breath.

'What is it now?' she asks, piercing me with her look.

'One guy wanted to kill another. That was five minutes ago.'

'I'm not your live-in maid,' she says, picking up a coin from the pile on my bedside table. She puts it in the slot, grumbling all the time.

'Thanks, darling.'

From behind, in that tight gown, she doesn't look so big. In fact, she looks pretty good. But she's still a bit old, thirty or something.

'Snotty-nosed kid,' she says as she turns around.

'Look, that's the guy who wanted to kill the other.'

'What do you mean? He's playing the piano!'

'That's right!'

She gazes at the screen for a minute. I don't think she's all that annoyed. I sometimes have the feeling I can see things no one else can. If only I could talk the way I think, say everything that's going on inside my head, I'd be pretty irresistible.

'Watch him play. He's getting ready to kill the other because he doesn't like the fact he plays better than him.'

'It stinks of tobacco,' she says. 'It's like a pigsty in here. If you carry on smoking, I'll have a word with the floor manager.'

She slides the cigarette butts under the table with her foot and then marches off, delivering a parting shot from the doorway:

'Turn the volume down! This is not your house, you know.'

'I once knew a tailor who killed somebody,' the old man blurts out in a hoarse voice, as if he were talking in his sleep. I had to put the mute on the pianist.

'You what?'

'A tailor who killed somebody. Well, he didn't do it himself, but it came to the same thing. It was during the war. He claimed the other was a Red, so they came for him in the night and he turned up in a ditch with a bullet in his head. Only the tailor was left.'

'The bastard! What did the others do?'

I pick up the remote. I know what the others did. A couple of days passed, and then they went to have their measurements taken for a wedding or funeral. On another channel, they're showing *Recordman*, my favourite game show. There are a couple of guys drinking water. It's incredible, the way they drink. They must have downed about three litres. The presenter urges them on.

'It was during the war,' says the old man.

'Would you look at those guys? They're going to burst!'

It's hilariously funny. Suddenly, one of the contestants looks frightened and stops drinking. A recordwoman – one of the hostesses, who look great and always have a breast showing – leads him off. The guy tries to smile, but I think he has water pouring out of his ears. There are only two left. They glance at each other as they gulp down liquid from a measuring jug. Between them stands the presenter, who reminds them there's a million up for grabs. The audience claps. The contestants carry on swelling, their misshapen heads on a level with the recordwomen's impressive twins.

It's back-achingly funny. I glance over at the old man to see if he's enjoying it, but he's fallen asleep. He must be in a really bad way to fall asleep at this point. I'll have to retransmit the programme later to Luou, who'll go 'mmmmmmm'.

I finally got them to give me Something. Someone came in, and I stopped sweating and being cold and thirsty. A nurse – not Miss Cowbutt, but Madam Mope – changed the sheets and pillows. I'd chucked up everything. The noodles resembled pale, defunct worms. I'd been through a really tough time. When the fireworks went off, I remember the old man kept saying, 'The boy's cold, the poor boy's cold!' To anyone who came in or went out.

'The boy's cold, the poor boy's cold! He's been shivering for an hour.'

I'd been telling them the same thing ever since I'd been admitted. It keeps happening, why don't you give me Something? They must have thought I was trying to trick them. I'd been several days without Something and without the *Sentimental Recordings*. They'd probably had a word with my mother and decided against it, but what they didn't know was that my mother lives in the clouds.

It was after dinner. I think it was the fault of that silent clock. Everybody started moving. They collected the trays with plates. Voices could be heard in the corridors. Heels receding into the distance. That was when I noticed the clock, its growing, noiseless din. The tiniest spring creaked like a mattress, and the minutest wheel advanced with railroad traction.

'It's making a lot of noise,' I said to the old man. I could hear my voice echoing, booming in the corridors of my head.

I breathed slowly and deeply. Rhythmically. This sometimes works, it gives me time to find a way out. But I only managed to chain myself more tightly to that infernal machine. There it was, opposite me, on the wall, getting bigger and bigger. I started throwing hundred-peseta coins, which rolled like tanks over the tiles. I was sure everybody had left. There was someone who, at a certain time, would come to lock up the hospital with an enormous key, of the kind used in medieval castles, and then stride off into the rain, their lantern swaying from side to side, climb into a boat and disappear into the mist of the bay. I had tears in my eyes, but couldn't cry, and this caused me pain. I took a deep breath and hurled the remote, which smashed the glass of the clock like the window of an armoury.

The Morning

Everyone is being very nice to me. Miss Cowbutt looks really amazing. I don't think she's wearing much under that gown, and her breasts are like those of a recordwoman. Her face is round, her hair short and curly, she has large eyes full of light, of the kind that glistens in wet fields. Now they've given me Something, I fcel a lot better. They've taken the clock away. I don't think anybody particularly liked this device for scaring away the hours because they haven't brought another, and all that's left on the wall is a yellow mark. The hours in a circle, with their ancient hooves. She's there, on her feet, checking the old man's temperature. He looks a bit yellow – or is it the morning light? – his white hair all ruffled, the curls glazed in sweat.

'It was very cold last night,' says the old man.

'It was,' she says.

'The boy was right.'

'He was. Does your leg hurt?'

'I can't feel a thing.'

I would feel like a king if only I could make contact with Help. Someone must have one of those mobile phones. Why didn't I think of that before?

'Let me see,' she says, pulling back the old man's sheet.

'Listen, darling.'

'You're not turning on the television,' she says, suddenly looking very serious indeed.

'That's not what I meant,' I reply, but she's already left.

'No, I can't feel a thing,' says the old man. 'Funny, isn't it? Yesterday it hurt like hell, and now it's as soft as a rose.'

He smiles thoughtfully. He looks younger, as if old age had taken refuge in the white thicket of his eyebrows.

'How are those bugs, captain?' I ask in order to show I'm also fighting fit.

'Animals are good creatures. They don't deceive you.'

I hear a commotion in the corridor. It must be my mother, lugging plastic bags and bad news with good intentions. She'll have learned about last night and will enter the room with bulging eyes and a stifled gale in her throat. But no. It's two hospital porters with a gurney and a doctor behind, who looks all stiff and formal, his hands in the pockets of his gown, wearing large, square glasses. Miss Cowbutt follows them in. She doesn't even look in my direction, but shows Mr Square Glasses some pieces of paper.

'Let's see what's going on here,' says the doctor in a calm voice, approaching the old man's bed and examining his leg.

'It doesn't hurt any more,' says the old man with a melancholic smile. I think he's a bit taken aback by the size of the retinue.

The doctor listens to his chest with that device they always carry around and then has a really good look at one of his eyes, using a magnifying glass and lifting his eyelid. I wouldn't like someone examining my eye like that, all on account of my leg.

'Is the family here?' asks Mr Square Glasses. He asks the nurse, not the old man.

'They're far away, there's so much to do...' he replies, as if apologizing on their behalf. 'Is there something wrong with my leg? It doesn't hurt any more. Not a bit.'

'We're going to have to take another look inside,' says the doctor calmly. I know that voice. Somebody always adopts that voice at difficult moments. He sticks his hands in his pockets and leaves, followed by the lengthy procession. I can hear the old man in the corridor:

'Are you going to put me to sleep again? You know, I'd really prefer it if you didn't.'

The Daughter

I'm just glad that my leg is hurting. I haven't used the call button, nor do I plan to. My mother was worried my leg was hurting, and I had to explain to her in secret what happens here to people whose legs don't hurt. Just as I thought, someone had told her about the previous night and, since she'd forgotten the *Sentimental Recordings* again, she went scurrying home to fetch them. She left in tears, having sworn I would break her heart one day, but not before she'd broken my skull.

The old man's daughter also came. She didn't find him in bed and started looking around, thinking he'd done a runner or something. She was about to poke her head into the bathroom when I informed her he'd been taken away.

'His leg wasn't hurting, and they took him off in a bed with wheels,' I said, convinced I wasn't expressing myself as I should.

I noticed that the daughter looked almost as old as her father. It struck me that the gold in her tooth was dirty and grimy. She was wearing a very ugly raincoat, tied at the waist, which made her bottom look enormous. And yet she had an outstretched neck like that of a plucked chicken and a tiny head, which glanced around in confusion, with bulging eyes.

'They took him off?'

'That's right. A whole load of people came and took him away.'

'Oh, heavens above! Was he in a bad way?'

'No, nothing was hurting.'

She put her umbrella and bag on the bed and left the room. I could hear her running.

Luou never receives visitors. He must feel pretty happy, lying there, in his spacesuit, without having to talk or eat or anything like that. I watch the saline solution going down and imagine nothing sliding down the course of his blood and breaking up into tiny, invisible droplets that settle at the end of his toes. The bastard. Perhaps in a couple of days he'll be lucky enough to have Miss Cowbutt spoonfeed him his soup.

'Luou?'

'Mmmm.'

'How are you feeling?'

'Mmmmmm.'

'Does your head hurt?'

'Mmmm.'

'And your arms?'

'Mmmmm.'

'What about your legs? Do your legs hurt?'

'Mmmmm.'

'Lucky you! Try to make sure it stays that way.'

'Mmmmmmmmm.'

I asked the splendid Miss Cowbutt how the old man was doing.

'What? Are they going to give my mate an operation?'

'They already have. You shouldn't talk about him like that. Who do these things belong to?'

'He is my mate. We've spent a lot of time together. He's a good guy.'

'He's not very well, you know. The situation is complicated. Who do these things belong to?'

'But is he really not well?'

'Yes, he's really not well. Have you any idea who left these things here?'

'Would you put a coin in the telly. There's an NBA game.'

'You like basketball as well?' she asked in disbelief.

'I like everything.'

The Walkman

My mother is a walking disaster. She returns with inflamed eyes, I bet she hasn't stopped crying for an hour and a half, how embarrassing, the taxi-driver asking her things or offering his condolences or just driving while looking in the rear-view mirror, there are some who have forgotten how to speak. On the bed, she opens that enormous bag she carries around with her, which must weigh a ton, full of medicines, receipts, empty biros, family photos, in one of which I'm riding a circus elephant. My ears are wide apart, and I look so petrified it's almost funny. My mother rummages around inside the bag. I know she has Something – Valium, Stabilium, stuff like that to help you sleep, or not to sleep. She pulls out the walkman. Good.

'How about the *Sentimental Recordings*?'

'The devil's recordings. Take this.'

'But what the hell is it?'

I can see her hands are inflamed as well.

'What the hell is all this shit?'

'Everything was in a real mess!'

I feel like bursting into tears. She's selected stuff from the drawer where Nico keeps all his Sunday-driver tapes. I go through the whole menu: that dumbo Madonna, great hits from the year dot, the soundtrack to *For a Few Dollars More*, one by a fat guy called Plácido Domingo – I'm not surprised – and a pop version of Mozart. I feel like chucking up. I can feel myself going green.

'They're tapes, aren't they? They were all mixed up, so I took a bit of everything.'

I can feel the tears brimming in my eyes.

'God damn it! I told you, I told you the *Sentimental Recordings* have a violet background. Even the dumbest idiot knows the *Sentimental Recordings* have a violet background and a skull.'

'I was in a hurry. I didn't have time to stop. The house is in a real mess. At work...'

'Have you any idea what this is? It's a pile of shit! Shit that Nico picks up at petrol stations. The *Sentimental Recordings* have a violet background and a skull.'

'Don't talk about your brother like that!'

'They were all nice and tidy. They're the only tidy thing in the house!'

'There wasn't any gas. I had to throw out a piece of steak!'

The tears finally come. I can see her in the kitchen, sniffing at the steak. Then throwing it away, a piece of limp, purple meat. I can see her making the sign of the cross – 'by the sign of the Holy Cross' – before she puts the lid back on the bin.

The Crutches

It's a strange feeling. I've done ten lengths of the room. In the beginning, I had a whole crowd of admiring spectators. I think my mother felt proud, even though I couldn't pay her much attention. I still can't believe she forgot the *Sentimental Recordings* again. For some reason, she hates everything I need, everything I love, which she calls 'Stuff You Pick Up When You're Out'. I gave the crutches a go to the rhythm of *For a Few Dollars More*. With the headphones, on stilts, I must have looked pretty impressive. Miss Cowbutt kept gesturing with her hands for me to slow down. I thought about giving Help a call, but was stopped at the door. Tomorrow then. I shall leg it down the corridor. Though it's pretty tiring using the crutches. Especially for the arms. When I finally calmed down, I almost couldn't hold the remote. It's funny, this happens to me sometimes, you can't stop the trembling in your arms, and your hands, fingers and everything start moving of their own accord, as if someone else were pulling the strings. I lay, staring into space, until the sensation went away.

'He doesn't eat anything,' said my mother.

'Oh, he eats, he eats,' I heard Miss Cowbutt reply. With

every passing day, she looks more and more like Kim Basinger.

'Then I don't know where he puts it,' said my mother.

I was the King. They were talking about me. Was I thin, or super-thin? I could see the blue blood working its way down the pale underside of my arm. I like my arm, so different when you turn it around – hairy and weathered, or bluish and fleshy.

'You know? Deep down, he's a good boy,' said my mother. 'It's all because of the company he keeps.'

My mother says 'It's All Because of the Company He Keeps' or 'Stuff You Pick Up When You're Out' with special emphasis, as if she were quoting the titles of some famous films. She and I are in the stalls, but for some reason my seat is empty and she looks around anxiously for my shadow.

'I don't suppose anyone has a hundred pesetas?'

I put on the headphones. I love watching telly, listening to my own music. Without the TV voices, with the music turned up, you see a lot more, you notice a lot more. They do that on *Hiroshima*. They show boxing fights or car races without any commentary, with the music turned up loud, and people are glued to the screen. You're perfectly aware what's going to happen, that guy who looks great, glistening with sweat and bouncing about in fluorescent shorts, is going to fall flat on his face. If there was someone talking – one of those commentators saying, for example, that he was born twenty-six years ago in Chicago, in a poor, African American family, and stuff like that – we wouldn't notice the fear in his eyes, the fact he's going to fall down. It's the same with racing cars. You feel a bit jinxed, leaning comfortably on the bar, with Something in your body, you go and say, I don't know why, that guy's going too fast, he's going to end up in the shit, and then he leaves the road on a bend, trailing a wake of fire across the ground, which is green already, and some guys in fluorescent caps, holding fluorescent extinguishers, with others carrying a stretcher, more slowly, go after him, but the driver emerges on his own two feet, staggering like a drunkard, gazes into the camera, and you realize he also knew what was going to happen.

Something else that happens when you watch telly, listening to loud music, is you can switch channels without any worries, because everything fits with everything else. It's fantastic. There are a couple of guys, they look like politicians because they're all wearing ties, and thanks to the music it sounds as if they're saying something important, their faces look important, you glance at their hands, which they move with practised precision, like a magician. You know they're going to raise their forefingers and point at you, but suddenly – bam! – you press the remote, and a colony of penguins in the Antarctic turns up, saying hello and goodbye in their stiff morning coats. Bam! Now there are cartoons, a mouse throwing dynamite at a cat, which blows up but, by the time it comes back down, it's whole again, so the mouse runs to hide. Bam! There's a game of American football, the players like neatly ordered gladiators. Bam! Then people, lots of people, thousands of human beings eating potatoes in a large field decorated with potato garlands.

The Phone Booth

I place a call, only to be told Help isn't there. What's worse, a girl who sounds like she's in a hurry, chewing gum or something, says Help doesn't exist any more, he's been taken off the air.

'Taken off the air? Listen, Miss Whatever-You're-Called, this is number 345, and I should like to speak to Help from *Sweet Dreams*.'

There is a silence. Miss Whatever-She's-Called seems to be arguing with someone.

'Just a moment please, I'll put you through to the linkman.'

This is all very strange. Before now, you only had to place a call, and there would be Help, saying hello with an echo that sounded like 'he-e-llo'. Now I'm waiting for some madman, some link in the chain, so to speak, a kind of chain fence, who's going to try and fob me off. But no. It's Help's voice, without the echo.

'Hello, friend.'

'Help, it's me, Sam, number 345.'

'Hello, Sam.'

Help's voice is muffled, as if it's coming from a funeral. I must have got '*Today, sadness*'.

'You can't imagine, Help, what happened. It turns out...'

'Listen, I can't talk right now. I have to put in a couple of slots.'

'Slots, Help? Ha, ha! Stop messing around.'

It's clearly '*Today, indifference*'.

'Listen, Sam, that business with Help is over.'

It's Help on the line. It's certainly his voice. But at the same time it's not him. How can that be? *Today, end.* It's too much. I feel a twinge in my leg and change position to lean on the other crutch.

'I had an accident, you know. I'm calling from the hospital. From the hospital! Don't you think that's funny, Help?'

'There is no more Help,' says Help's voice with a hint of impatience. 'That programme doesn't exist any more. RIP. Over. Have you got it?'

'Hey, listen up for a moment! You are Help! What is it, Help, what's going on?'

'Goodbye, Sam.'

Behind me is a long queue of people waiting to make a call. They don't look very well. The one nearest to me has yellow skin. He looks as if he's going to talk to someone in the other world.

'Just a moment,' I say so he won't come any closer while I search for another coin. 'Just a moment, right? It's very important, a matter of life... There it is! Help? Is that Help?'

The disgusting Miss Syllable-Eater is back on the line. I hear 'Help' and 'nothing'.

'Listen, Miss Whatever-You're-Called, could you go a bit more slowly? I'm lame, you know, and can't follow.'

She hangs up.

Tip and Top

I've taken a liking to *For a Few Dollars More*. It helps me walk. I adjust the headphones, grab hold of the crutches and confront the long corridor. This trip to the phone booth is the first I've undertaken out of my room. I almost had to hop, in search of Help, my friend Help, Help the traitor, the bastard. The return is looking like a real punishment. I'm sweating. The crutches squeeze my chest like a pair of pitchforks. How could I have been so stupid? When my leg is healed, I'll head over and stuff the *Sentimental Recordings* down his throat, one by one, starting with '*Today, friendship*'. Or else I'll go with my crutches and, at the first blow, Miss Gum-Chewer's head will roll across the floor like a snooker ball, ending up at the feet of that swine, who'll look up with an astonished expression, and I'll say, 'It's me, Sam, remember, Help? Come on, Help, why don't you play me "*Today, happiness*"?' And then, bam! Another blow to the back of the neck, another ball rolling across the floor, one less dunghill. I feel like throwing up. Why's the floor leaning like that? It's so damn bright. There's a slap on my shoulder, and I turn around.

Tip and Top! God closes one door and opens another. I think it's the first time I haven't had a problem remembering one of the proverbs my mother repeats a thousand times. This, and the one about rams always mating in January, which she said only once when flicking through a gossip magazine and then claimed not to have said. It's Tip and Top, smiling, in tracksuits, each holding a can of Coca-Cola.

'Hello, mate!' says Tip. 'What on earth are you doing here?'

'My leg!' I reply, holding up my crutches as triumphantly as I can. 'My leg, ha, one is going to be shorter than the other, ha, ha!'

'That's amazing!' says Tip.

'No way!' says Top.

My heart is leaping for joy. If Tip and Top are around, then Don can't be far off. And, wherever Don is, there is always Something for his friends.

'Don's here, you know?' says Tip in a whisper, winking surreptitiously.

'Yeah, he's here,' says Top a little more loudly.

'Don's here?' I ask, unable to suppress so much happiness.

'He had an operation for appendicitis!' says Tip, as if this were an extraordinary event.

'For appendicitis, ha, ha!' says Top.

'Appendicitis? Ha, ha!' I laugh as well. I'm never quite sure what this is, but I know people have an operation and it's obviously hilarious.

'Do you want to see him?' asks Top.

'I sure do!'

I'm dying to see him. My whole body is trembling with the possibility of seeing him. The floor has stopped moving. It's shining brightly like the sky.

'Can you walk?' asks Tip.

'Can you move?' asks Top.

'Walk? Just watch this!'

I take several long strides. The crutches seem to have been inspired by my excitement.

'Come on then! We'll have to go down in the lift,' says Tip.

'In the lift, that's right, ha, ha!' says Top.

Don

Tip knocks and then pokes his head around the half-open door. Don likes people who are polite, people who talk quietly, people who eat without making too much noise. Don is always eating something, soft things that look a little transparent, and his hands are like inexhaustible pantries, replenishing anthills. You think he's finished, but then he stuffs something in his mouth and carries on chewing. With Don, you always feel like eating.

'Is there a problem?'

'Oh no, Don! No problem,' says Tip, grinning like a rabbit. Don hates problems. Whenever there's a problem, he stops chewing, and his flabby face grows tense.

'A friend, Don!' exclaims Top gleefully over Tip's shoulder. The two of them look dumb. Nobody would ever guess that they're the Company's most feared henchmen.

Don is extremely fat. The fattest of the fat. He's almost in the dark, leaning on some cushions, only the reflection of the television casting a pale light on his face. He looks like a Buddha. It's not quite clear whether he is sitting or lying. Can they really have opened up his stomach without him deflating?

'Well, if it isn't our friend Sam, what a surprise!' says Don. He talks very delicately, like a girl playing with her dolls. 'Come in, come in. What's that you have there? Don't tell me you have a problem!'

'No problem, Don,' I say with my best smile. I know he knows. 'A stupid accident.'

'You have to take care, Sam. Cars can be a real nuisance.'

'One leg is going to be shorter than the other!' I say in a happy voice.

'Well, isn't that funny?'

'They're going to call me Sam the Lame! Ha, ha!' I laugh, and everybody else joins in.

'I like you, Sam. I like your character. Come, come and sit over here. So what happened?'

I tell him the truth. You always have to tell Don the truth. If you act cool with him, he'll act cool with you. And, wherever Don may be, there is Something. I mean Something Real.

'You're a good guy, Sam. I wish I could give you Something. Something Real. But I'm a little concerned.'

He knows I know what he's referring to.

'You have nothing to be concerned about, Don.'

'Listen, Sam,' he says very seriously, 'you haven't shown your face in a while. Are you not my friend any more, Sam? Why didn't you come to see me?'

'I don't know, Don, I had some kind of problem...'

'I hate problems, Sam. You've no idea how much I hate problems.'

'I know, I know, Don. I'll pay you what I owe. I'll pay everything, Don, everything.'

'I'm sure you will, Sam. The boys,' he says, pointing at Tip and Top, 'were getting a little anxious, but I said to them, "Calm down, Sam's reliable, he'll pay up soon enough."'

'I will, Don, I will. When I get out of here, I'll come around and pay you everything.'

'That's good, Sam, that's good.'

I grab my crutches and get up from the bed. I'm feeling slightly dizzy. Don's face keeps changing colour in sync with the screen. Now it's pink. No, green.

'Why don't you have Something, Sam? Something from a friend.'

He slips his hand under the cushions and places Something in the pocket of my pyjama jacket.

'Come back whenever you like, Sam. I like your visits. You're a fun guy.'

'Thanks, Don.'

'Goodbye, Sam.'

Barbara

I took Something Real and felt like I was in heaven. Everything, including the ambulance sirens, reached me as a soft, pleasant sound. I could hear myself breathe, follow the air through the labyrinth of my chest and then go out with it in a slow exhalation, like the smoke of a tranquil fire, the flight of a seagull, the flutter of a flag.

I suppose I should give Something to Luou, but it might be better if I keep it all for myself. I haven't abandoned him. I devote a few minutes each day to him, but he just keeps on sleeping. Stuck in that spacesuit of his, he seems to be spacewalking all the time. Or else driving, peering over the steering wheel, on a long, solitary, straight road that glistens after the rain. Who knows what's going on inside his head?

'Do you want me to read to you, Luou?'

'Mmm.'

'How about something horny?'

'Mmmmm.'

'Listen then. "To start with, they kissed and caressed each other softly, their bodies moving slowly, in mutual exploration. Suddenly, Barbara opened wide her eyes, as if she were climbing a mountain and, on reaching the top, had found the mouth of a volcano. What had really happened was that Sammy had grabbed her marvellous tits in his powerful hands and started pounding her with an energy she found so unbearable she stuck her nails into his buttocks. The unstoppable beating of his pelvis opened her fanny to impossible limits."'

I pause and gaze in amusement at Luou's expression. His eyes are also wide open. I think he's going red as a beetroot. These magazines are really too much.

'Mmmmmmmmmm.'

'So you want me to go on? "Barbara was so open, when his prick went in to the end, she could feel the wonderful tickle of his bouncing balls." Ha, ha, can you imagine, Luou? "Sammy stopped for a moment with his rod out, still pressing down on her tits, just enough to feel Barbara's embrace, the anxious yearning of her vagina. He thrust in his prick again and heard the pleasure-filled moan in Barbara's throat, as if the head of his penis had come into contact with her vocal cords." Ha, ha, so what do you make of that? Listen now. "For Sammy, this was an unmistakable sign that he was winning, pumping her fanny relentlessly, and she was so given over she felt herself dying." Can you imagine, Luou? The girl felt herself dying! "'You're going to kill me, you bastard, you're going to kill me,' said Barbara. 'Take this, Babs, take my prick,' shouted Sammy. And at this point she screamed, 'Ooooh, David, David!'" Fuck, Luou, did you hear that? The girl was thinking about someone else when she came.'

We look at each other in confusion. I suppose we must have adopted the same expression as Sammy when he heard her cry, 'Ooooh, David!'

'If that happened to me, I really would kill her, don't you think, Luou?'

'Mmmmmmmmmmm.'

The Umbrella

Recordman today, it has been announced, is going to be more intellectual. It's a question of using your head. The contestants, a couple of men who look like primates in their Sunday best, have to knock down a wall of breeze blocks with their heads. The first one to do so will get a million. The gong goes, and they all rush to the wall. From the initial impact, one of them, the one who looked most hard-headed, falls flat on his face and is looked after by two recordwomen, who today are wearing tight, discreet dresses, though they do have a hole right over their nipples. The audience claps. Unbelievable! This is great.

'Grandpa, would you look at that?'

I was just about to say this, but the words got stuck in my throat before I looked around. There, in the corner, next to the door, is the umbrella lying on the plastic bag. It's a long, black umbrella, of the kind that never gets left behind at bus stops or in train stations, those large, desiccated crows villagers drape over their shoulders, with the wings folded in.

The contestants smash into the wall, and the recordwomen show their mauve nipples. Everything strikes me as brutal and stupid. I like it. I wish something real would happen, they'd break open their heads and breasts, and a hotchpotch of bloody male brains and female milk would spatter against the screen. I press the remote. An indigenous child in Peru, sick with cholera and wrapped in a colourful shawl. I press the remote.

Horses racing down a strangely deserted road. The advent of the ecological car. I press the remote. A huge crowd eating a humungous potato omelette. What do I care about the old man? Once the coin has finished, I'll go and see how he is.

The Coffin

She's down below, hunched in the leather armchair, as if she were never going to get up again. Her head is bowed, and she's clinging to a tissue. When did her teeth start falling out? Has she always had the inklings of a moustache? Once upon a time, she must have been young, sucked honey from her father's thumb and opened wide her eyes when he mimicked the cuckoo.

'Cu-ckoo, cu-ckoo! Cuckoo be damned!'

The old man has died. In his place in intensive care is someone who's been patched up after coming off the motorway.

'Was he a relation?' asks a nurse.

'No, he wasn't.'

I say he wasn't, but feel bad about it. I didn't even know his name.

The dead in hospital are put in freezers in the basement. People joke about this because that's where the kitchens are. In the room where relatives wait, it's cold as well. The walls are bare, there's just the poster of a skeleton and a no-smoking sign, which reminds me of the need to smoke. The daughter, a wreck, glances up for a moment with inflamed eyes. I don't know why, but people look less stupid and less ugly when they cry. Standing next to her, two men are discussing the subject of money.

'We'll take care of everything for a hundred thousand, transport included.'

'The other one,' says the man in a black tie, pointing outside, 'will do it for seventy thousand.'

'Those bastards! You know they're illegal, right? It wouldn't be the first time they've been stopped by the police and the deceased has been returned without a coffin or anything.'

'Well, they say they can't come into the hospital, but after that it's no problem. All we have to do is bring the dead man to the door.'

'Listen now. Don't go complicating your life. Take a look at this,' says the man in rolled-up sleeves, producing a catalogue, 'now that's a real coffin, *Elegance on Your Last Journey*, complete with metal crucifix and carved edges.'

'Yes, but the difference is thirty thousand.'

'We'll throw in a wreath. A wreath of carnations with a violet ribbon and golden letters.'

'Andrés, I want him to have a crucifix,' interrupts the daughter in a serene voice.

'A fine coffin, this one. I don't like to sound pompous, but the truth is you only die once. If you could just sign here. Do you have a car? Shall we arrange a car? All right then. Here as well. If you could just sign here as well.'

The man with the papers quickly leaves past where I am

standing, and the one I assume is the old man's son-in-law walks towards the far wall, staring at the tips of his shoes, with his hands in his pockets. The daughter doesn't take her eyes off the steel door. I decide to introduce myself and tell her how sorry I am.

'Hello!'

She looks up in alarm, as if the devil on crutches has come in, but attempts a smile as soon as she recognizes me.

'Hello, boy.'

'You forgot your umbrella, did you realize? And a large bag.'

'He died like a little bird,' she says and bursts out crying.

'The nurses kept asking who they belonged to, and I told them to leave them alone, they belonged to you.'

'Look, Andrés, it's the boy from papa's room. He was very fond of him. Really very fond.'

'I said no problem with the umbrella, you would be back for it.'

'Papa said, "He's not a bad boy, no, not a bad boy."'

She's far away, buried far below, calling me 'child' and things like that. I don't feel like saying goodbye. It's as if the heating has been switched off. I think to myself the old man's in there, in only his pyjamas, dying of cold, and there are probably animals hanging up as well, which have been slit open.

'How's the dog?' I ask. I don't know what else to say.

'Did you hear that, Andrés? The boy asked about the dog!' she exclaims, on the verge of bursting into tears again.

'The dog? How the hell do I know?' replies the man, shrugging his shoulders.

'What do you mean, how the hell do you know?' asks the woman in surprise. 'The other day, you said you were going to let it go.'

'And I did let it go!'

'You let it go? Then where is it?'

'I let it go. I let it go. What else was I supposed to do? I couldn't get a wink of sleep after your father left.'

'You let it go? Now he mentions it, I don't think I've seen the dog since.'

'I let it go! What more do you want?'

The son-in-law moves away, muttering under his breath, 'Just what I needed! Someone bringing up the subject of that blasted dog...!'

'Right then. Well, I just wanted to say not to worry about the umbrella.'

'Thank you, child,' she says. I catch her glancing at her husband with contempt. 'Thanks for coming.'

The lift is full of old, sick women in slippers and pink dressing gowns, coughing and covering their mouths. One of them looks at me. She has two grey clouds with black birds in place of eyes and, behind the tired squeaking of the lift, I can hear, 'He's not a bad boy, no, not a bad boy.'

My Brother

If there's something I cannot bear, it's being called a 'twat'. It makes my blood boil. I don't know why. Call me something else, and I won't mind. But not 'twat'. It makes me feel like a gob of green spit someone treads into the ground. And Nico knows this.

'Twat!' he says as soon as he arrives. 'You're a twat!'

'And you're a son of a bitch!'

He stares at me as if I really were a disgusting, grey-green gob of spit and walks towards me with a deranged look.

'I'll kill you! In God's name, I will!'

I can't breathe. For a moment, I think he's going to do it, he's serious. His robotic pincers almost suffocate me against the wall. Nico never loses control, but this time he's gone crazy and I think he's foaming at the mouth. My mother finally starts crying, and then he lets go.

'Now you're going to tell me who you gave the ring to.'

The Ring

Nico must have driven all night. I always thought that country of Basques, who lift large rocks and want to become independent and sometimes place bombs, was very far away. But no, he's here in a split second, a mass of biceps holding me in the air like a rag doll. They're not Nico's eyes, but those of a replicant from *Blade Runner*.

They bore into me like laser beams. Perhaps at police headquarters they're subjected to radiation to make them immune to rocks and bombs.

'Where's the ring?'

'It wasn't worth anything! They told me it wasn't worth a penny!'

All that hullabaloo just because of my mother's wedding ring. I took a hundred thousand pesetas, what she earned for sewing thousands of stupid beads on to fancy outfits, I took the video, Nico's special gift for the house, and those other jewels my mother wore only once a year. But she was beside herself when she noticed the ring was missing, that tiny bit of wire. I'd never seen her like that before, so dejected, without enough energy to tell me off, sobbing so much she could hardly breathe. I swear I imagined it was all because of the video. Really, I thought about it a lot, but I had no other option. I couldn't risk bad relations with Don. It's only a loan, mother. I'll give it all back. You'll see. That's what I wanted to say.

'What do you want me to do? Go out and steal? Is this what you want?' I said finally. It was a point of view that sometimes worked.

I also would have liked things to be better organized, to be able to get to Something with elegance, without being such a loser, with the mafia where it had to be, and things like that. But you only have to look at the facts, what misery. Assaults on paralytic old ladies, lonely Labradors, bankrupt shopkeepers, schoolchildren. I've seen films in which gangsters are people with style. They live in mansions with porches full of parrot cages and bougainvilleas in the garden, gardens with blond-haired girls on swings, doing deals while playing golf and controlling the situation with clever one-liners such as 'don't let your feet go in front of your head' or 'look after the little fish, but don't let their teeth grow too big'. I would have liked to work with people like that, but what I got was Don, that fat man in patent-leather shoes. I took him the picture from the living room, a painting of Christ by Salvador Dalí, and he burst out laughing.

This time, however, my mother did not calm down after crying. She went and called Nico. All she did was talk to him about the ring, that blasted wedding ring. I could always go and get it right now, but I don't want to appear in front of Don with problems for a while.

'Bilbao police? It's Nicolás' mother here. Nicolás Castro. Could I speak to Nicolás?'

'He didn't come at the time of the accident, and you're going to make him come now?' I said to her from behind, but she didn't want to listen.

'Nico, son, it's me...'

I needed Something and shut myself in my room. When Nico arrived this morning, I'd forgotten all about it, but he was insistent I should remember, and so was my mother, as if there hadn't been a night in between.

I'm wearing my black T-shirt with a red dragon on the front. Nico hands me my white jacket.

'Put this on!'

Only when we're inside the police station does he let go of my elbow. I'm expecting a whirr of walkie-talkies, a constant procession of officers in bulletproof vests, the metallic sound of handcuffs, the rattle of typewriters machine-gunning bits of paper, plain-clothes detectives crushing cigarette butts in ashtrays, but there are only two uniformed policemen chatting unenthusiastically about football and a bald man at the back, who looks like some kind of clerk, blowing his nose. Nico introduces himself, and the man says something about the weather.

'Here's the boy,' says my brother. 'Samuel.'

The man gives me a blank stare. He doesn't say hello or anything. He takes a tissue and wipes his nose.

'Let's see then.'

He gets up and leads us to a map of the city on a cork board. There are different coloured pins. That drawing is somehow familiar. The city is shaped like the head of a dinosaur submerged in the sea. The red pins are concentrated like a collar around the animal's neck, where the brown on the map is less intense and green patches appear.

'Here's the rubbish dump,' says the bald man. I imagine thousands of seagulls alighting on his finger. 'What can you see there?'

'Before you reach the dump, on the right, is a kind of shack.'

'Several shacks.'

'There's one that's surrounded by empty bottles. There should be an old woman sitting outside.'

'An old woman?'

'That's right, an old woman with lots of skirts, sewing. If the old woman is there, you have to go to Labañou. There's a shop, a shop that never opens.'

'What does it sell?'

'Batteries, headlights, things like that. There are also motorcycle helmets and... a cactus. Like that one,' I say, pointing to the window.

The bald man listens carefully. He seems to be enjoying the details and doesn't want the story to end. This makes me feel relaxed. It's a film, and I'm starring in it. I can hear children playing with a ball and a woman hanging out the washing, singing, '*Si vas al cielo azul, al cielo azul, yo voy contigo.*'

'The shop's always closed but, if the sign says "Open", then you can continue.'

'Continue? Where?'

'To Portiño, a fisherman's shed. If you don't show your face in all the other places, there won't be anyone there.'

He gazes thoughtfully at the map for a couple of seconds and then hurries to his desk to talk on one of those antiquated phones, which are large, black, and have a white dial. He only dials one number. His nose isn't running any more, he's handing out orders. He looks like a real superintendent. I'm so afraid I burst out laughing.

The Dump

Nico drives the car. He's wearing a denim jacket and looks a lot younger, twenty or something. In fact, I think he's much older than that, about twenty-five.

'How old are you?'

'You what?'

'How old are you?'

'Twenty-six,' he says bad-temperedly.

'Twenty-six? Blimey!'

We climb the road to Bens, in the direction of the dump. The ditches are full of rubbish that has fallen off the dustcarts. Bits of plastic have wound around the gorse and brambles like pennants from a party in the past. There's a very green field – strangely green, since everything in that place is usually dusty and smoky – and, right in the middle of the grass, the red shell of an old car, with two empty holes where the headlights should be. It looks like the skull of a diplodocus. Diplodocus were herbivores.

'It stinks out here!' says Nico, and he closes the window.

There's a great view of the city. From this height, it looks quite small, a lengthy outcrop jutting out into the sea, a cement puzzle on its back and the tower with its bulging eye at one end. The ships and cranes resemble toys. If you stretch out your hand, you can move the heaps of coal and gravel, the piles of wood and slate, along the quay. The oil tanker entering the bay, being pulled by three pot-bellied tugs, measures from bow to stern the same as my thumbnail.

'I've no idea whether this is going to work,' I say to Nico. 'They don't know the car. Or you either.'

'It's better they don't know me. Just stay calm. And do what you always do.'

There's the old woman, in a cloud of shit, with her rags, sitting in front of the shack, which is held together by planks and metal patches and surrounded by empty beer, wine and champagne bottles. A granny at ease, enjoying the sun from the rocking chair on the porch of her country home. Nico stops where I tell him to, and I get out. I look for a stone and throw it at the seagulls. They launch wearily, lazily, into the air, followed by a petulant pair of choughs. On the other side of the road, some Gypsy children are playing with a rust-ridden fridge. One of them gets inside.

'I need a cigarette,' I say, going over to Nico's window.

'I don't have any tobacco.'

'Shit! What do you mean, you don't have any tobacco?'

'No, I don't. I don't smoke,' replies Nico, looking worried.

'Then a butt from the ashtray. Something. I smoked the time before,' I say, rummaging in my pockets, 'but don't have any with me.'

I light the butt. Only the filter is left. Disgusting. When I get back in the car, I'm coughing my lungs up.

'It's what I always do.'

Nico appears serious and looks at his watch. Before we get to Labañou, I ask him to stop at a bar.

'I'm going to buy some tobacco. And take a leak.'

'You need to take a leak right now?'

'It's not a question of choice.'

Two workmen in blue overalls come out with a sandwich. The bar is deserted and almost dark. At the far end is a slot machine playing the music from *Star Wars*.

'Do you have a phone?'

The Operation

'A-OK,' I say to Nico, having passed in front of the *Atlantic Accessories* shop window. The sign says 'Open', but the door is firmly locked.

Nico glances at his watch with a professional air and opens the glove compartment. There's a walkie-talkie with red and green lights.

'Attention, Season! Sparrowhawk here. Do you receive me?'

'Season here. Very well. Over.'

'Everything OK. We're heading back to port. Over and out.'

'Understood, understood. Over and out.'

'Right. Let's do this,' says Nico, taking a deep breath.

It's great. For a moment, I think the car is going to accelerate, jump like a horse and lift its nose, with only its back wheels for support. But no, it creeps forwards very slowly.

'There might not be anybody there,' I say, lighting another cigarette.

'If it's as you said, then they have to be there,' replies Nico.

'Yeah, right. Well, it's always worked before.'

Before heading down the slope to Portiño, Nico stops the car.

'If they're not there, we're going to have problems,' he says, staring into my eyes. 'Most of all, you're going to have problems, Sam, do you understand?'

'Listen here for a moment. I did everything I had to. I can swear it. Why don't you ever trust me?'

'All right, all right. Are you ready?'

Everything happens very quickly after that. Nico honks his horn three times. It's then I realize there is a procession of patrol cars behind us. We race down the slope, piercing the air with a wail of sirens. The cars screech to a halt, forming a barrier that blocks access to the wharf.

'Now, Sam, run, run,' shouts Nico, giving me a push. 'Which door is it, which door?'

'The green one. No, the blue. No, no, the green.'

'The green one, the green one!' exclaims Nico.

Two policemen kick it down while the others form a cordon around the shed. It's pitch-black inside.

'Police, nobody move!' says the superintendent. He waits for a moment and then switches on the light.

There are nets piled up, and fish baskets in small, triangular heaps. On the right, a table and three chairs are all the furniture. One chair has a tyre as a cushion. On the table is a lamp, a magazine and an ashtray.

'Leis, take a look around,' says the superintendent, flashing me a glance.

'It's one of those cultural magazines,' says the plain-clothes detective with a hint of scorn. 'What an educated lot!' In the ashtray, there are only some raisin stems.

The wharf is deserted. On the surface of the sea, among the rocks, a carpet of buoys bobs about. The superintendent walks towards the breakwater with his hands in his pockets, and the seagulls clear a way for him with hysterical laughter. He then comes back.

'Take the boy, Castro,' he says, gazing at the moving dots of the bay. 'We're going to catch ourselves some velvet crabs.'

The Plate

'Eat,' says my mother. 'Even if it's just a boiled potato.'

We're sitting peacefully, communicating with the tinkle of our spoons, when the news breaks on TV. The police have discovered a large shipment of Something in waterproof packages hidden inside some fishing nets. Nobody has been arrested, but the investigation is ongoing.

'We're leaving for Aita tomorrow,' says Nico to my mother.

'Who is leaving for Aita?' I ask.

'You and me.'

On TV, they're talking now about an attack in the Basque Country. Someone has flown through the air when about to start his car. It must be very unpleasant to die like that, with such a shock, when you're still half asleep and your dreams are fighting not to melt away with the morning frost. All disembowelled cars, all dead people, look the same. The street always looks the same, and the shoe that has fallen on the pavement is also the same. A car, a dead man and a shoe that look as if the cameraman has put them there.

My mother jumps in the air and switches off the television.

'The two of us. We're both leaving for Aita,' says Nico slowly.

'Hey, just a minute! What's going on here? I'm not going to Aita. I don't feel like going there at all.'

'We're both leaving for Aita,' says Nico, and he carries on eating as if nothing has happened.

'You may be, but I'm not.'

I decide that now is a good time to escape that accursed plate and put an end to the argument, so I get up from the table.

'Eat!' says my mother. 'You're all skin and bone, can't you see?'

'Sit down!' says Nico.

'Hey, what is this? I don't want to eat. I don't want to go to Aita. And I'm leaving the table. Leaving. All right?'

Is this Nico? Whoever it is, they grab me by the neck and ram my face on to the plate. I try to push against the table with my arms, but feel like a defenceless bird. All I can do is blow out. The water of the soup forms bubbles and ends up splashing everywhere. But Nico won't let go. Why aren't you crying, mother?

'You're going to eat and you're going to go to Aita,' says the animal.

Aita

Of my mother's seven siblings, none is left in Aita. And yet they spend the whole day talking about Aita. Aita this, Aita that. None of them gives a damn about the place. The only ones that live there, in the stone house, are my grandmother Herminia and a bitch named Princess with eyes like a cow. The house is full of flies in summer. Thousands of stupid flies that collide with the yellow strips hanging from the ceiling, next to the light bulbs, the animal fat and laurel branch. The more flies get stuck there, the more flies replace them, as if they were giving birth while stuck to the trap. Flies in the milk, in the red wine, in the soup bowl. Flies searching for something on your skin. On one particular day in autumn, the flies leave and the rain comes. The air starts to billow around your feet. The animals turn watchful. There's something going on inside the stone and wood. Suddenly, on the summits of Faro and Castelo, the imperial army appears. In a rage to start with, firing cannons and bolts of lightning. Then in the form of gusts riding the wind, which for months has been hiding like a bandit behind Regatiños dos Congos. Later, stubborn and tame, it occupies the screen until you tune into its frequency, a swollen sadness. That is when you hear the lamentations with piercing clarity. Damn place, there's nowhere to hide. The pulley of the well, the axe for cutting wood on the stump, the cart, moos, traps, bells, crows, distant engine, the night in the mouth of dogs and the old people calling out to children.

'Samueeeeeeeeel. Nicoláááááááááás.'

'They're calling to us.'

'Sh, don't make a noise!' said Nico, covering my mouth in the attic. 'Remember we're aliens.'

The Horn

My mother is at the door and hands me a bag. I give it to Nico, who grabs it and heads outside, muttering under his breath. I know what's inside their heads. Hope. I bet they've talked about it and got to the conclusion there's fresh air in the mountains, and peace, and silence. They have no idea how ill it makes me feel just to think about Aita. There was a time, I think, when I was happy there. I'm riding the wicker hurdle, sitting like a miniature fakir on my grandmother's shawl, and can see the cows' enormous, elephant-like bottoms. I'm lying on the cart's green bed, wrapped in a sack that smells of flour. Someone hands me an open pomegranate. Something went wrong, something irreversible, so that now I can only think about the cold in Aita.

'I'm going to die of cold, you'll see.'

'Don't be daft,' says my mother.

'Fuck me!'

'Can't you wash your mouth?'

In the past, she would have given me a kiss and told me not to go down to the river alone. I had sweets for the journey and a change of clothes, fur-lined Wellington boots and a pair of pyjamas with embroidered anchors and ship wheels. She would lovingly have pinched my cheek – back then I had proper cheeks – and told me to be good. Boh! I probably replied, 'Yes, mother.'

'It's in the back of beyond!'

Nico beeps the horn. My mother slams the door shut. I look at the light well. It wouldn't be difficult to escape, just a single leap. Nico beeps the horn. My mother opens again. She's already in tears.

'Are you still there?'

'I'm going, God damn it, I'm going!'

'Don't talk like that.'

That idea about running away was a stupid one. I can imagine the scene: me freezing in a doorway with Nico twenty yards away, asking, 'Have you seen a boy who's half lame?' 'Yes, he asked me for money, but I didn't have any spare change.'

'You can sleep if you like,' says Nico, fastening his seatbelt.

'Fuck it, man, I've only just woken up.'

'Don't talk to me like that! I've had it up to here with you.'

'Jesus, man, I'm not a machine.'

I light a cigarette just as Nico winds down the window and puts on his sunglasses. Where does he think he's going? I don't remember the last time the sun shone in these parts.

'Patience, man. I'm not a machine. I can't just program myself and say, "Out with swear words, ptah, ptah! They have been eliminated from my system." I'm not like you.'

'Don't push me!' says Nico. His forefinger looks as if it's about to shoot, on a level with my nose. 'I'm going to say this once: don't push me! Enough of your messing around, got it? I'm losing two weeks of my fucking vacations because of you. No more messing around, got it?'

The accelerator brings to an end any attempt on my part to protest. Who asked him to give up two weeks? What do I have to do with this pointless cruise to the hell of Aita?

'You're an addict. You're seventeen and up to your neck in shit. Why don't you fucking wake up?'

An addict, me? What's he talking about? It's a nice, grey day. The city smells of freshness, as if somebody has opened all the sewers to the sea.

The Ditch

There was a time I got on very well with Nico. Really well, I mean. Just thinking about it makes me want to weep. Nobody could touch me. I would say I was going to tell Nico, and nobody would dare touch a hair on my head. Back then, Nico was one of the Red Devils and had a black-and-yellow-striped jersey he wore on Sundays.

One night, there was an open-air dance in Mallos and he came back very late, it might have been light already, with traces of blood on his nose. Nico kept quiet. He didn't utter a word of complaint. My father hadn't gone to bed and, when Nico arrived, he took off his belt and started beating him.

'I don't like this.'

'What don't you like?' asks Nico.

'Travelling here, in the passenger seat. All you see is the ditch. Have you noticed the number of disembowelled dogs there are in the ditch?'

'Go to sleep. Why don't you go to sleep?' he says in a calm voice. This voice suits him very well.

'I can't sleep. Not in the car. I don't know. I always dream I'm being dragged along by something. Sometimes it's because I've fallen off a horse, which has bolted, and I can't get my foot out of the stirrup. Other times, I'm tied to a sledge, which is being pulled through the snow by dogs, and the snow burns like embers. I dream I'm travelling on a bus, my seat sinks, nobody realizes, the others are asleep, and I end up sitting on the tarmac. Ha, ha!'

'Right,' says Nico, also laughing. 'Dreams can be incredible.'

'What do you dream about? I mean, do you have any recurring dreams?'

'I don't know... I suppose so. There's a call I always have to make. A phone call. I'm aware of it the whole night, I know I have to place that call, but things keep happening, I get distracted, people invite me for a drink, I know I have to place that call, but always end up getting involved with something else. By the time I wake up, I still haven't placed that call. I don't know who it's to, but I haven't called them.'

'Dreams are fucking unbelievable.'

'Right.'

Nico looks funny in those sunglasses. A cattle truck lifts a wave of water in front of us. Aita will be a mud-bath, grandma will be blowing on gorse sticks to make a fire.

'Is it true they program you?'

'You what?' he says in that voice I don't like.

'I said is it true they program you. You know, you do brain-control exercises and things like that.'

'You must be mad.'

'I read something like that. For example, not to be afraid. The heads of policemen are programmed not to be afraid, and that's it. That's fantastic!'

Nico changes gear and overtakes the cattle truck. For a moment, we can't see anything. Just a curtain of water sliding down the windscreen. As he overtakes, Nico purses his lips.

Oasis

That solitary house by the roadside has a red lantern and a sign on the front with a drawing of two palm trees and the word 'Oasis' in blue neon lights. A German shepherd, chained to a kennel, barks at the cars, dripping in the rain. At one of the barred windows, a woman looks out. It's less than a second, but I see her face, as if it's pressed against the windscreen. The woman has black hair, with curls falling over her forehead. She stands staring at me until the windscreen wiper erases all trace of her.

The Car

As we enter Terra Nova, there are several road signs. The first is triangular and shows the silhouette of a cow. The second, also triangular, shows two children with school bags, holding hands. The third is circular, with a red border, and says '40'. Judging by the amount of overtaking, I would say everybody uses this opportunity to accelerate. Terra Nova is the kind of place where nobody stops unless they have to. Nico stops.

'It's the gear disc,' says the car mechanic. His glasses are as thick as the bottom of a glass. His eyes are so big it makes you dizzy just to look at him. 'You're in luck. That kind of thing can leave you stranded.'

'I noticed something strange. There was no power when I changed from third to fourth.'

'*Capisco,*' says the man in the oily overalls. He has the air of a delirious sage.

'So when will it be ready?' asks Nico.

'We'll have to order the part. This afternoon perhaps.'

'This afternoon? What time?'

'The part has to come from Coruña.'

I head for the door. I have the impression crows stop in Terra Nova out of compassion, to give it some warmth. The cold in Terra Nova can be seen. Its flight is circular and heavy. It doesn't enter the houses, but emerges from them, from the half-built rows at the roadside. In one of the apartment blocks under construction, whose brick ribs are visible, bare-necked chickens scrabble about.

'The car's not well,' I said and shouldn't have said it.

Nico stares at me now from the end of the refrigerated warehouse. He doesn't move from the dismantled car, as if watching over a defenceless man on his last legs. The mechanic with the diabolical glasses is both short and large. He rubs his hands on dirty rags that make them blacker every time he does it.

'Don't worry, my friend. The car's in good hands,' he declares, slapping the bonnet and imprinting his fingermarks.

'This afternoon,' repeats Nico in a regretful, but demanding tone.

'Yeah, this afternoon. Possibly. Ha, ha!'

In Terra Nova, there's a bar-tavern-restaurant-inn-grocer's-ironmonger's-videoclub. It also serves as a toyshop, since there's a doll dressed up as a fairy and a couple of pistols with a sheriff's badge in the window. On the sign, it says 'House of Novelties'.

Cornelius

Only one voice replies to Nico's 'hello' when he enters the *House of Novelties*. This belongs to an enormous man with a strange face, neither old nor young. I watch him closely as I play on the space invaders machine. Actually, what I have to shoot down are not space invaders, but Chinese-looking dwarves in cricket shells, which proliferate on the screen after each missile. The giant over there clearly never combs his hair, long locks that twine around his ears and down his back like ivy. He talks to himself, standing at the bar, in a ventriloquist's hoarse, deep voice, and takes large slurps of brandy. He has a very loud voice. Up in one corner, the telly, a couple reproaching one another. And my machine going 'pow, pow!'

'So I said to him you take it.

'What the hell!

'I should have taken it!

'For goodness' sake.

'You take it.

'My currency knows no fear,

'my destiny is only to suffer,

'T-o, To, Toooro, Toooro!'

'Keep it down, Cornelius!'

This is one of the old men, not so old, playing dominoes. There are four of them at the table. All fat, smoking cigars, except for one, who has a toothpick and a sunken face.

'What is it, Cornelius, you feeling sad?'

The landlord, bald and pot-bellied, forces a smile when I go over to Nico, having dispatched a whole consignment of dwarves, but not enough to get a free game.

'Cornelius, hey, Cornelius! Are you on the moon, Cornelius?'

'Oh dear!'

'Leave him alone, why don't you? Have another, Cornelius. It's on the house.'

Nico asks the landlord if we can eat something. Everybody turns towards him, as if this is the first time anyone has asked to eat in that place. The truth is it does say 'restaurant'.

'Maybe,' answers the landlord finally. 'But it's still a bit early, don't you think?'

'It's two o'clock. Well, almost,' says Nico, looking at his watch.

'A bit early,' remarks the landlord.

'So what time can we eat?' asks Nico.

'Later. A bit later.'

'Do you have any tobacco?' I ask. 'Blond tobacco?'

'He has everything. E-ve-ry-thing!' replies Cornelius before the landlord has a chance to speak.

The Axe

Nico orders a beefsteak, and I order egg and chips with chorizo. The landlord goes away, muttering under his breath, and comes back with a large bowl of boiled potatoes, turnip greens and pork.

'Eat this!'

'Where are my eggs?' I ask. All I can think about is dipping my bread into the oily juices left by the eggs and chorizo fat.

'It doesn't matter. This will do fine,' says Nico.

The landlord then brings over a jug of red wine and soda. I recall having ordered a Coke, and Nico said he wouldn't mind a beer.

'I told him to stick the money up his arse.

'In whose name would I do such a thing?

'No way!

'Poncey gentlemen!

'Stick the money up your arse.

'That's what I said.

'Legionnaire, legionnaire,

'whose bravery knows no compare,

'T-o, To, Toooro, Toooro!'

'Keep it down, Cornelius!'

'They're all off their heads,' I whisper to Nico. 'Raving lunatics!'

'Sh, just eat and keep quiet.'

Having finished our lunch, we watch some cartoons. It's pouring down outside. From time to time, people come in, and their large, black umbrellas, leaning against the counter, form puddles in the sawdust. One local buys a birdcage. Another, a mousetrap. Another – a thickset man in a corduroy jacket, with a blond moustache and white beard – an axe. The customers' conversations merge with Cornelius' monologue, the slapping of domino pieces on marble and shots being fired at Bugs Bunny. Who on earth buys an axe at three in the afternoon? I'm convinced, as soon as he leaves, the man with the blond moustache and white beard will head straight to the forest where the lucky rabbit runs and cut Christmas trees.

The Fight

Nico spends the whole afternoon toing and froing between the *House of Novelties* and that warehouse where the corpses of cars are kept on ice. I have finally got the landlord to crack open some Coca-Cola bottles and am alternating between space invaders, telly and the bar's dramatic scene. Cornelius' monologues become increasingly twisted and provocative. He seems to be fighting everybody in the air and can only find a pleasant face in that glass he hasn't let go of since we arrived.

'Knife, not wolf.

'And the judge swallowed.

'Twin-breasted woman of ill repute.

'Nobody sang in the village.

'Everyone can be whatever they like,

'my previous life doesn't matter,

'T-o, To, Toooro, Toooro!'

'Keep it down, Cornelius!'

It's getting dark. People stamp their feet as they enter the *House of Novelties*. Finally, there's a little warmth, as if all the cold has gone outside. You can see the cold's face of a tramp in the first flashes of the headlights. Nico is soaked.

'Bastards!'

'What about the car?'

'They're saying now they don't know when it will be ready. The whole afternoon, leading me up the garden path.'

'Uh-oh! I told you they were all crazy around here.'

'We'll have to stay the night.'

'You what?'

'We'll have to sleep here.'

The domino players must be celebrating a world championship. A huddle of spectators has formed around them. The players themselves are sprawled out, studying their moves from a distance. Whenever it's their turn, they lean forwards, brandish a piece threateningly in the air and then bring it crashing down on the table. From time to time, one player gets angry, stands up and walks towards the door, spitting out curses. A terrible tension arises, and it seems everybody is cocking their weapons under the table. But then he comes back, sits down and laughs out loud. Quarrels are always between teammates, never with those on the other side. It's funny. I suppose this only ever happens in dominoes and cards, when players are comfortable. On an open field, the fight is always against the enemy.

'Do you have any rooms?' asks Nico.

'We might do,' replies the landlord.

'And we'll need to have dinner.'

'It's still a bit early.'

'Yeah, right. Is there a newspaper?'

'There might be. It's from yesterday.'

'It doesn't matter.'

Inside the telly, it isn't cold at all. It must be nice and warm. Everyone is scantily dressed and looks content. Through the door, wearing a pair of diving goggles, walks the car mechanic. He greets all those present. He seems like a happy enough guy. Suddenly, I see the giant leaving the bar and approaching Nico, who is reading the paper.

'Hey, you, aren't you going to drink anything?'

'No,' says Nico, looking up in surprise. 'I don't feel like it right now.'

The landlord is drying the glasses with a white cloth and watches in amusement from behind the bar. On the domino table, the slamming of pieces grinds to a halt.

'I don't feel like it!' exclaims the giant in a mocking tone. 'You're not from around here, are you?'

'No, I'm not,' says Nico, going back to the paper.

The giant doesn't give up. He's really very big. And goddamn ugly. He's frightening, with those sunken eyes between mounds of flesh. He places an enormous hand on Nico's shoulders, and I can hear the bones crack.

'You're not from around here, are you, my friend? And you don't like what you see. You don't like Terra Nova, do you?'

'I'm reading, if you don't mind.'

The others laugh through gritted teeth. I can see Nico's eyes flashing. I imagine his muscles are tense, like those of a cat.

'Well, do you like Terra Nova or not?'

'Would you just leave me alone?'

'Leave me alone, would you? Did you hear that? Did you hear how he speaks?'

Nobody says anything. They seem to be enjoying the spectacle. Only the landlord murmurs, 'That's enough, Cornelius, that's enough.' The giant turns the screws a little tighter.

'Where are you from, shitface? Don't you think Terra Nova is pretty?'

Nico leaps to his feet, overturning the table to gain space. He bares his teeth and raises his arms. I know what he feels like – a Red Devil. I'm waiting for him to do what he has to do. I gaze at the audience in triumph. There you have him, my brother. Something holds him back. The other's eyes are virtually white and seem to be looking nowhere in particular. Nico lowers his arms, sets the table straight, picks up the newspaper and goes back to reading. Everything else follows: the space invaders, the television and dominoes.

'That's enough, Cornelius! It's time you went home,' says the landlord.

The giant grabs a metal-tipped walking stick and staggers out of the bar.

'We're all unknown heroes,
'let no one seek to discover who I am.'

I watch him disappear into the watery night.

'Car's ready,' I hear the mechanic telling Nico. 'That's what I came to tell you. Good as new!'

My Grandmother

Welcome to Aita! This is peace. The night sliding over the shadows. The earth gurgling in the yard, beneath the carpet of pine needles. Attention!

'Owwwwww!'

'What are you doing? Have you lost your mind?' says Nico, rummaging in the boot of the car.

'Listen.'

It never fails. All the dogs in Aita start barking in order. First, Princess, who's next to the granary. Then, one after the other, the Brandarices' dog, the Lousames', the Pancorvos'. Who knows how far the chain reaction will spread? Perhaps one of the barks will cross the Grande river, and those in Somonte will reply, followed by those at the mountain limits, over in Quincá. A two-legged guy who's just arrived does a poor imitation of a wolf, and all the dogs in the universe start barking as a result. When the guy falls quiet, satisfied with the effects of his tomfoolery, they carry on doing the same, getting more and more worked up, like sentinels who've fallen into the enemy's trap and are now reproaching one another. Were it not for the dogs, Aita would not exist at nightfall. It's incredible how the darkness clings to the stones when it rains. I can't even see Nico. At the far end of the yard, the door to the kitchen opens, revealing my grandmother's silhouette, framed like a little saint, with that weary halo cast by the lights of Aita. How on earth can she see us? She needs glasses just to sew and read.

'Careful now! It's muddy. *(You don't say, grandma!)* No, no, my boy, don't tread there. *(Crikey, she was right!)* That way, right there, where the trough is. *(How on earth can she see?)* No, Nicolás, not there. To the right. Behind your brother. That's right. *(Got it, dumbhead?)* And what time do you call this? *(If only you knew!)* It's not going to stop! *(It sure as hell is not.)* It didn't rain yesterday, well, not so much. *(Same old story.)* Come on in. Over there, where the fire is. Over there, by the fireplace. That's right, where it's nice and warm. Are you hungry? *(No.)* You must be feeling hungry. *(No.)* You'll want to eat something. *(Nothing at all.)* It'll do you wonders. *(No, it won't.)* Just one little plate. *(Or two.)* Or two. *(To start with.)* That car is new, isn't it, Nicolás? *(How on earth can she see?)* I thought so from the sound. *(You must be kidding!)* Nando bought a new car as well. Nando, Daniel's son, the one who works in a bank. *(Of course he does.)* Come on, eat. *(Ugh!)* Did you stop in Terra Nova? *(You know we did, grandma.)* People are very strange over in Terra Nova. *(How on earth does she know all this stuff?)* Come on, Samuel, eat, you're all skin and bone. You're going to put on some weight in Aita! You'll soon see how you put on some weight in Aita. *(Finally, we look at each other, and I can see her face, white as flour, like the faces of Chinese actresses constantly carrying things, dashing about on their knees.)* I haven't done a thing today!'

'How could you, in this weather?' says Nico.

'Nothing. I haven't done a thing.'

She stokes the fire, cuts a slab of bread and comes and sits next to us on the bench, a plate of potatoes on her knees, everything nicely ordered, her floral apron like a tablecloth.

'I haven't done a thing all day.'

'I'm going to buy you a television, grandma,' says Nico. 'It'll keep you company.'

'The Lousames have a television. But you can't see a thing. Because of Faro.'

'Because of what?'

'The mountain. It casts a shadow, and you can't see a thing. Well, just a couple of lines.'

The Storm

The mice don't stop scrabbling about in the attic and sky. Little mice feet pattering over the ceiling. Enormous mice steering fighter bombers through the clouds. Mice gnawing inside my head. Bright mice eyes glinting on the windows, between the geranium pots. Nico snoring like a huge mouse stuffed with maize, between the sheets. Where is there Something to go to sleep? I know grandma has things you can take in the sideboard. She must have Something. All houses have Something. I slowly descend the stairs. The bolts of lightning cling to my naked feet. Downstairs, the embers of the fire also look frightened in the corner.

'Is that you, Samuel?'

'*(Jeepers creepers!)* Yes, it's me, grandma.'

'What is it, child?'

'I just wanted a glass of water, grandma. A glass of water.'

'Are you afraid, Samuel?'

'*(I'm terrified, grandma, I'm dying of fear!)* No, grandma, of course not.'

'Do you want to come to my bed?'

'*(I'd love to, grandma!)* What nonsense, grandma! I just wanted a glass of water.'

'Come on, into my bed.'

My Grandfather

This is Aita. A graveyard with a church surrounded by houses. To get from one place to another, people sometimes take a shortcut past the old gravestones, which have crosses that are different from today's, with suns behind, moons and stars, and things that look like tools. By the side of the church, the stone sarcophaguses sometimes act as benches or troughs – those that don't have a lid – with green water where frogs sleep. One day, we caught an eel with a string of worms in the Grande river. It took the bait, and its teeth got caught long enough for us to give it a pull and throw it on the grass. It was like a wet snake in Nico's hands. We put it in a sarcophagus, the narrowest one, which must have been made for a slip of a girl, since it was called the virgin's. People on Sundays, before attending Mass, would prod the eel with a reed. And we would stuff it with worms, pink worms from manured land.

No, it's not far to go when you die in Aita. You close your eyes, are taken from bed and laid to rest just a few yards from your door. When you look out of the window, you can say hello to your deceased relatives. We've played marbles on our ancestors' gravestones. The marbles roll over the dates and names and sometimes get stuck in the dot of an 'i'. Samuel Castro Ti(nes). I can hear him down below, 'Won't you keep quiet for a minute?'

'He's just a boy, Samuel, can't you see he's just a boy?' says Grandma Herminia.

'Then let his parents deal with him. Did you see what he did to the crabs? Any day now, he'll set fire to the place.'

'He's just a boy. Can't you see he's just a boy? Come here, come to grandma. Do you want a little sugar?'

All things considered, the dead of Aita have it lucky. My father is in Feáns, the municipal cemetery, on a fifth floor at least. My mother used to take us at All Souls, and Nico would clamber up a ladder with a bunch of chrysanthemums. We haven't been in ages, but my mother still goes.

The Bread and the Fish

I am woken by a loud blast from a horn. A beam of light filters through the half-open shutters. I feel terrible, sleeping doesn't agree with me. A hundred years could have gone by. The horn sounds again. What's that idiot Nico doing? But no. It's the bread. A smug-looking man in a white apron gets out of the van, holding a pair of scales. During the delivery, the whole group – the baker with his floury hands, the women's grey hair, the breath coming out of mouths – everything is sprinkled with a light the baker's effeminate hands deal out in pieces. Where did that sun come from? They never used to deliver the bread. You had to go to Timor to get it. I was sent once. I ate the whole thing, an entire loaf, on the way back. I stuck a finger in the mass, and it was warm. So I carried on digging. No sweet ever tasted so good. I remember I wasn't told off.

When the baker leaves, the sky grows dark. You can see the air's shadow running through the grass. Then there's another horn, two short, penetrating blasts. The woman from the fish van is blonde and has rolled-up sleeves. There are fewer people now, and they don't form a circle, but come up one after the other, staring into the boxes, sniffing with their noses. One points, and the blonde woman pulls out an octopus, holding it by the base of its head. The tentacles hang low, limp in her arms, which are solid and tense like a man's. The octopus is now the colour of stone, of the gravestones by the church. When it's cooked, it will be the red colour of a woman's hair. Grandma follows my gaze. Crabs move about in one of the boxes. I know she's going to buy them. What happened before: I found them in a bucket in the kitchen sink, took the bucket to the granary and emptied it on top of the corncobs. There they were, an expedition of strange creatures with spindly antennae and periscopic sights, traversing mountains of gold. I made them fight with my plastic soldiers.

The Mirror

The dampness has entered the mirror as well and unfurled black ivy along its edges, where the spider has woven its web. I am caught. Everything passes slowly before my eyes, bringing dry leaves that land on me sleepily and carry words and memories of others. This is Aita. A goddamn cobweb. I look at myself in the mirror and pretend to be a monster.

The Potatoes

'Did you go to the Brandarices' house?'
  'I did. *(You know this, grandma.)*'
  'And did you go in?'
  'I did. *(You know this very well.)*'
  'And didn't they give you a bad look?'
  'Actually no. They just came and went. I spent the time with Gaby.'
  'It's strange! Ever since that girl came with her baby, they haven't spoken to anyone. They're always in a bad mood, as if they're under a curse. They never ask for help. They don't attend Mass. They only go to funerals, but stay at the back, by the door, and leave before the blessing. The old woman, Amparo, hides from me, pretends not to see me, but I carry on talking to her all the same.'
  'Why, what happened?' asks Nico, trying to glimpse the front of the neighbours' house through the window

above the kitchen sink, in between the sprigs of parsley.

'The girl, the one your brother spoke to, came back with a child,' says grandma, peeling potatoes.

'Gaby has a baby,' I pointed out. 'You remember Gaby?'

'Yeah, sure.'

'Well, she travelled around, Europe and places like that, and came back with a baby.'

'There are worse situations!' exclaims grandma. 'That's what I said to Amparo. Nothing. They're so ashamed. Heavens above! As if their souls had departed from their bodies. And then there's the child, poor thing, they say the child's a shrimp, a little potato... Damn these potatoes! They're all withered, not worth a thing!'

Grandma pulls out their eyes, the white sprouts, which look like mole feet. So wrinkled, hands and potatoes seem made out of the same material, wrapped in the same skin and stained by the same earth.

'When do you plant potatoes?'

'Around March.'

The strip of potato peel tries to wrap itself around the back of her hand until it falls off like a snake's old shirt.

'Around March,' says grandma. 'If there's still someone to plant them.'

The Nut

Gaby, Gabriela, pulls back the little blanket as if it were the petal of a flower and reveals a baby the size of a toad. The baby, which is the size of a mouse, gives off a gleam, and I wonder who could cry for such a thing, since a baby the size of a worm could hardly invoke a bolt of lightning on its own.

'Don't you think she's beautiful?' says Gaby in a whisper when that gram of life finally stops wailing.

'Yeah, she's beautiful.'

She's horrible. To tell the truth, all babies are horrible, with those wrinkled dwarf faces. It's just that, to make matters worse, Gaby's baby is the size of a fist.

'She's so small!' says the mother. 'I sometimes think I'll pull back the blanket and she won't be there, an eagle will have snatched her in its talons, or something like that.'

From time to time, you still see eagles in the skies of Aita. But there are far more crows. Were there more eagles, there would be fewer crows. Eagles are warriors; crows resemble outlaws, wandering free, in the wilderness, with no thought for the present or future. In the fields where rye is planted, farmers don't put scarecrows any more, but outlaws hanging from a stake by their feet.

'They're not crows or anything!' I hear Gaby's father say in a rage. And he continues, 'I don't know where all these crows come from. You keep on shooting, but they just reappear, as if you're firing into thin air. Do you know how much a single cartridge costs? They're not crows or anything. I don't know where the hell all these crows come from.'

I stretch out my hand, and Gaby's baby grips my forefinger with its capuchin hands. Someone must be applying strength on the baby's behalf. It's the size of a blackbird.

'She was premature, born at seven months,' says Gaby. 'She spent days in an incubator. It was a miracle she survived.'

Gaby's child is a girl. I know this, because she told me.

'I felt very sad when I found out it was a girl. I also felt happy knowing it was a girl, I don't know if you can understand me. I just thought, if it's a girl, it won't survive.'

Gaby is beautiful. She looks like a woman, so sad, staring into nowhere. The fingers of her hand are as long as bamboo reeds. I let go of the baby and stroke it. What I really want to do is let go of the baby's fingers, which have fastened on to me like needles, and stroke Gaby's bony hand. I let go of the baby's fingers and glance at my watch.

'I'll never leave this place,' says Gaby. 'I want her to grow up here and pick cherries.'

'Do you... do you fancy Something, Gaby?'

'You what?'

'Oh, nothing.'

Princess

Princess is on heat, and grandma has decided to lock her in the granary. The granary used to be full of corncobs, but now there's just old junk, pots and pans, cracked crockery, the handlebars of Uncle Lito's bike, pine cones, pine needles and the odd bit of firewood. Suddenly, half the world's dogs turned up in our yard. All the sentinels that protect the night of Aita were there – mongrels, short-tailed and small, which couldn't even reach the bitch's behind with their snouts and were the most obstinate, or large and glossy dogs, with an air of haughtiness, which kept their distance and acted like marquises that just happened to have been passing by. Grandma got tired of shooing them with a stick and decided to confine Princess, who seemed both flustered and flattered by so much attention.

'There! Take care of the child!' said grandma. And she threw in a deflated ball that had yellow butterflies on it.

Before this dog, there was another Princess in the house. A cow. Grandma tells me they have the same eyes.

The Moth

I can't cope with the night. It's stronger than I am. I sit against the bedhead, the cold of its metal bars digging into my back like those of a prison, and can't retreat any further. Night with its black cape peers in at the door and is only held back by the dusty glow of a bare bulb.

The moth also looks ill at ease, banging its head against the bulb. If I switch off the light, the moth will fold its wings and be consumed by fear. Nico is snoring. I wish I was programmed like him and could do what I had to at each moment, without hesitation, without second thoughts, without altering anything, moving in sync with the camera. I wish I could be like the people in that magazine Nico brought for grandma, actors posing next to their new partner in their new house, slender models on the catwalk, royal families on the stairs of a palace, the widow Caroline of Monaco in her mourning bikini, all so sure of themselves, so comfortable, they make me feel strange, a strange beast that jumps at the creaking of a hinge whenever the pages are turned. How can something as light as a page make so much noise, something like a moth with its velvet wings, the spring of a mattress, the air entering and leaving Nico's lungs, a mouse's padded feet? I know why cities were created. So we could forget our own noise, the unbearable little noises caused by fingers and fluttering eyelashes. I can hear the tumult of the street, the police sirens, the struggle of engines, the tuning of televisions, the ringing of phones, the neighbours' disagreements, and the night, in dismay, stops playing with the lock in that room in Aita. Like a forest plane, the jet from Madrid to New York passes overhead.

The Milk and the Apples

When the first light of day filters in, Nico is no longer snoring, but carries on sleeping with his mouth half-open. From downstairs comes the first sound of saucepans, water from the tap, and the smell of boiled milk. Grandma always lets the milk overflow, she lets it get burned, puts it back in the same saucepan, and it overflows again. When you pour it into a glass, it has a yellow colour and tastes old, like milk from another time. If I don't go downstairs, if I head towards the window upstairs, it smells of apples, dozens of apples lying on the floor, on top of blankets and rags. It looks like an enormous snooker table with a baize of stripes and diamonds, all worn and patched up, with balls that have lost their enamel and way of rolling, healing scars, accumulated and lonely in the half-light.

Dombodán

Dombodán's sheep graze in between the gravestones. There's also a donkey that stares at us with great interest and swivels its left ear about like a radar. Dombodán is seated with a staff in his hands, on top of the tomb of Adoración Dombodán Tasende, 'who died aged 41, on 11 April 1985, your sons Benito and Luis do not forget you'. Next to him, with a stringless guitar that has a flamenco dancer painted on it, is Dombodán's brother, the Blue Child, with his enormous, bald head and transparent veins. Dombodán doesn't speak, but nor is he deaf.

'Hi, Dombodán!'

'Ha.'

'Remember me?'

'Ha.'

'How is everything?'

'Ha.'

'How about the hunting?'

'Hu.'

It's a real pleasure to chat with Dombodán. You do the talking, and he agrees with a guttural sound full of various nuances, in which can be distinguished good, bad and so-so, big and very big, small and tiny.

'A boar?'

'Ha.'

'Was it big, the boar?'

'Haa.'

'What, this big?'

'Haaa.'

Dombodán isn't just any old hunter. It is said he can spend three days hiding in the undergrowth, on the trail of a deer, expressionless beneath the sky, wearing a hat with ear flaps, until the scent of man has evaporated and the animal grows confident.

'Three days, Dombodán?'

'Ha.'

'Three days is a long time!'

'Hmm.'

Dombodán is no fool. The fool of Aita, Manoliño, died when I was a child. I can still recall the funeral, never had there been so many people. Manoliño used to go around with a jackdaw on his shoulder, which could talk – well, it could say things like 'shit', 'bastard' and 'ore' (instead of 'whore'). The jackdaw landed on the coffin, and no one dared to shoo it away. As the priest intoned the prayers, the jackdaw pecked at the coffin and kept saying 'shit' while the people said 'amen'. Dombodán is something else. Over dinner last night, grandma agreed to tell us one of Aita's secrets if we promised to spread it about. Dombodán takes on commissions, special errands. He's something like Aita's guardian, its protector. He keeps an eye particularly on outsiders. Old people in Aita are afraid of hooded gangs from the city's suburbs that come and burgle village houses, stealing images from the churches. Listen up, you delinquents, should you ever see a shadow with ear flaps in the Aita night, know that this is Dombodán and he never misses.

Dombodán sticks his hand in his swollen trouser pocket. It must reach down to his knees. Who knows what might come out? It could hold a lamb at the very least. He produces a collection of trinkets on top of the stone. A knife, chestnuts, leather straps, pieces of string, egg-shaped pebbles, different-coloured cartridge cases, a torch, a rabbit's tail, a calendar with a supermodel in the nuddy ('ha!'), a calendar with the Virgin Mary, a Real Madrid key ring, bird feathers, glass beads, a lighter and a boar tooth. And a handkerchief, a coloured handkerchief that seems to go on for ever. He punches me on the shoulder and points at his goods.

'For me?'

'Ha.'

'You want me to choose something?'

'Ha.'

'Come off it, man! I couldn't do that. They're yours, understand? They're your things.'

The second punch is on the verge of dislocating my shoulder. Dombodán wants me to choose something in token of friendship, and I will have to make up my mind if I don't want to end up in a heap.

'OK then. The rabbit's tail. They're said to bring you good luck.'

'Ha.'

I suppose I should give him something in return. I rummage through my pockets. Not a thing, not even a penny. Dombodán points at my badge. The glorious star of the Red Army. It hurts me to part with such a treasure. Never mind. The donkey watches on in amusement. One ear is rigid, the other is limp, out of service. How on earth does it manage to move them separately?

'Look, Dombodán, look how I walk. One leg is shorter than the other.'

'Hmmm.'

The Flowers of the Dead

In one corner of the yard, near the cabbage patch, grandma has a little garden with a hortensia hedge, where she looks after dahlias, arums and chrysanthemums, flowers for her dead. She's bent double, and I can't see her. I can only hear the hoe loosening the soil. When grandma stands up, she discards a handful of weeds and puts her hands on her hips, pressing down on the knuckles. The women of Aita never spit while they're working the land. The men do. They spit on their hands and the earth.

The Cart

Almost everyone in Aita has a tractor. Lucas too. But Lucas only works with his tractor when it's a holiday. Other times, he uses a cart.

'This cart was made by your grandfather!'

Lucas' cart sings a lot. It makes more noise than a car. What I mean is that a car makes noise, but we don't hear it. We must have a special apparatus in our ears for not hearing cars when we don't want to. Carts, on the other hand, can be heard moaning as they approach, and continue to moan even after they've disappeared into the distance.

Here comes Lucas with a rope in one hand and a stick in the other. I know what he's going to say.

'This cart was made by your grandfather – may he rest in peace!'

Ever since I was a little child, the same old story. Today, coming and going.

The Revolver

Nico has spent the whole afternoon fiddling with the car engine. He keeps accelerating and decelerating. He looks worried.

'What's the matter?'

'With the car, nothing.'

'Ah!'

He then washes it very carefully. He strokes it with the sponge as if it were the back of an animal. I enjoy watching him.

'Why don't you lend a hand or go away? Do you have to sit there the whole time?'

'What's the problem? I'm not bothering you.'

Nico looks very serious. When he finishes, he gazes at the car in satisfaction. Then he buttons up the cuffs of his shirt and enters the house. When he comes out, he's eating an apple and wearing a jacket.

'I'll be back soon.'

'Where are you going?'

'I'll be back soon.'

'Can't I come?'

He adopts an irritated expression and walks off without a word. I follow him, whistling to make my presence known and to annoy him. He returns the favour by walking quickly. For the first time since I dispensed with my crutches, I have the impression I really am lame. He enters a burned forest. The grass, soft and light green, almost transparent, sprouts from a soil that resembles tarmac. I follow Nico's gentle zigzag as well as I can but, even so, the branches blacken my face.

'Blimey, we're going to get lost!'

'Nobody asked you to come,' he says without looking around.

'I understood you were here to keep an eye on me, you were my own private policeman.'

This makes him stop. He doesn't look at me with hate or a desire to box my ears. I think he has the kind of problems you get inside your head. I know all about that.

'Fair enough. Come on,' he says finally.

We leave the ashen forest behind and climb to the top of a hill. There are the remains of a fort, a ruined, half-buried maze. The damp earth has been scuffed up by BMX tyres. Down below – a Nativity scene – is Aita. With its mooing and crowing, its human voices getting tangled in the smoke of chimneys. The abandoned quarry on the other side of the hill is where the wind stops before galloping off. It still hasn't left today and neighs like a haltered stallion, its marine snorts echoing around the rock walls.

Nico collects some Coca-Cola cans scattered on the ground and lines them up. He then walks slowly backwards, opens his jacket and takes a weapon from his holster. I knew he had one, I knew he always kept a weapon close to his chest, but he's never let me see it, even at a distance. I imagined a pistol, a modern pistol, black, with straight lines, like Bond's. But what Nico has in his hands is a revolver, a real revolver, with its revolving chamber and curved handle, like those in westerns. Even so, he doesn't shoot with one hand. He spreads his legs apart and extends both arms to grip the weapon. When he fires, the wind falls quiet. The whistle seems to roll down the sides of the quarry.

'Let me have a go.'

'Here, you hold it like this.'

The Waterfall

On our return, we visit the Cerva waterfall. The water plays at drowning in water. It slides down rocks, vainly attempts to cling to reeds and then laughingly collapses on its bottom. In the riverbed, it opens wide its mouth and gurgles before finally vanishing in a whirlpool. It's a beautiful place, fringed by royal ferns and moss with long hair painted with carnival spray. An advert for men's cologne. We pee, standing next to each other. The roar quietens the river, we can hear our own spout, a little stream that foams and bubbles royally.

'Let's see who can pee the furthest!'

There was a time we were very close.

The Mill

We follow the river, from ruin to ruin, mill to mill. The mills haven't been used in years. The brambles peer in through the windows and crane their necks through the holes in the roof. The stones are tinged green, weeds sprout in the cracks and joins. On the wall of one of the mills hangs a calendar with a sailing boat plying rough seas. The pages with the months – the days in blue (except for holidays, in red), the names of saints at the bottom, in tiny letters – are stained by damp. The water sings underground but, if you pay attention (January, February, 1970), it's a storm heading upriver to seek shelter in the Congos mill. The millstone is still in the centre, clean and polished, almost gleaming in the half-light, as if waiting for the roof to finally cave in, so it can lift off in search of the planet of living mills.

'I'm going to take it,' I inform Nico, who stares at the floor and ceiling with distrust.

'Do what you want, but let's go.'

I leave with the storm under my arm, clearing a way down the blind alley of alders, until we reach the track to the fish farm. The water in the pools there is darker and makes you feel colder. When the valley flooded, they opened all the dams. Two days later, people filled their buckets with trout from the fields.

The Mother of All Trout

Before the old bridge, at a bend in the river, is the cave belonging to the mother of free trout.

'Stop mucking about!' says Nico. 'It's getting late.'

This is a large trout that only ever comes out at dusk, its green back flecked with black spots. Everyone says they're going to fish for the mother of all trout, but I don't recall ever having seen someone with a rod in those parts. Bits of blue plastic have got caught on the roots of the alders. Perhaps young trout build houses like those of emigrants from Terra Nova when they come back from Europe, replacing stone with tiles, wood with aluminium, slates with asbestos. I throw a few mint leaves into the water.

'Where are you, old woman?'

If she's still alive, I bet she has glasses for her weary sight and woollen socks to warm her feet.

Rosa

I suck the sweet quince juice off my fingers. Nico gazes at Princess Caroline in her mourning bikini. Grandma peels potatoes next to the fire.

'Whatever happened to that girl?'

'What girl?' asks Nico uneasily, without looking up.

'The one you brought round once, when you had that other car.'

'Oh, that was ages ago!'

'She looked very nice,' says grandma.

Quince goes very well with cheese, as if they were both produced by a cow. Nico turns the page. Grandma grabs another potato.

'She was very charming. She offered to sweep the kitchen floor.'

Cheese is spread on bread, quince on cheese.

'What was her name?'

'I don't know. Rosa. Her name was Rosa.'

'Rosa, that's it. Now I remember. She looked like a boy with that short hair and those jeans. She was very pleasant.'

Nico flicks through the pages. On the back cover is an advert for Martini with two glasses and a flower.

'I'm off to bed,' says Nico.

'You what? You haven't had dinner.'

'I'm not hungry. I ate all that cheese.'

'That's not enough! You have to have dinner. Otherwise, what's the point of peeling all these potatoes?'

'She was hot, that's what she was,' I say, sucking my fingers.

'Shut your mouth!'

'What's the problem? Can't I talk? She was very hot.'

'How about you?' asks grandma. 'Do you have a girlfriend?'

He

Nico is snoring. I'm not snoring, rather I'm holding my breath. I switch on the light and walk slowly towards the curtain of wooden beads that acts as a door for grandma's bedroom. No, she isn't snoring either, she's almost not breathing. I retrace my steps and listen again, kneeling on the carpet, my ear close to Nico's chest. *In, out. One, two. One, one, two. One, two, two.* That's impossible. Let me see. *In, out. In, in, out. Out, out, in.* That settles it. Apart from Nico, there's someone else sleeping deeply. And it's not me. My bed is unmade and empty. The hand covering my mouth is my own. There's nothing under the beds. I take the calendar with the sailing boat and listen carefully, but I can't hear anything, not even the distant storm echoing inside the conch shells. I press my ear against the walls. The further away I am from Nico, the better I can hear the other. I should wake him but, if I wake Nico for such a trifle, he's capable of tying me to the bed with his belt and dousing me with ice-cold water. I climb on to the metal bedhead, as close as possible to the ceiling. I can hear perfectly now. The other is asleep in the attic. I walk on tiptoe towards the window and feel the touch, the soft, clammy caress, of the apples. Down below, in the light of a lamp that sways in the wind, I can see the gravestones of Aita. People always joke that the dead return to their houses on stormy nights, when the tombs become flooded. But all the gravestones look in place, and the weather is much better than yesterday.

Who said anything about fear? My legs are trembling, but it's from the cold; my teeth are chattering, but it's from laughing. Where does Nico put that revolver when he's asleep? Under his pillow, perhaps, or between his legs – who knows? There's a torch on the mantelpiece. The trapdoor is in the large bedroom, where the family's six daughters used to sleep, including my mother. Come on, Sam, who said anything about fear? The torch's circular light goes in front, dancing happily over the linen mattresses. It finds the stairs. Light between the teeth. That's it, Sam, push with your head, a little harder, it's creaking, that's it, uuuuup we go!

The luminous eye scans the various objects in the attic like a spotlight and is thrown back in pieces by the broken mirror of a wardrobe. Nothing strange in sight. With half my body inside, I reach some corncobs on the floor and scatter them into the four corners. Not even the mice move, dozens of eyes on the lookout. That's it, brave Sam, we can return with our head held high, having fulfilled our duty. But – hang on a minute! What's that over there? Blow me down, if it's not the old radio, the one that used to occupy an altar in the kitchen! I raise myself fully into the attic and, full of emotion, approach the treasure, which sits on a disjointed chest. The box, made of wood, is so dusty you can draw a heart with an arrow on it. I write 'Gaby + Sam', then rub it out. I scrape my nail across the cloth of the loudspeaker, then turn the dial, which groans like the mechanism of a toy. What if it works? On the master beam, I know, there's a light-bulb socket. There it is. I rotate the bulb twice, and the attic goes a yellow colour inhabited by lazy shadows. My heart is beating ten to the dozen. My God, the light on the dial switches on! Gently, slowly, the sound of interference increases, like the song of cicadas in summer. I move the dial to and fro and suddenly come across confused chords and voices. A sentence in French. Dervish music. Someone discussing the origins of the universe in Robocop Spanish. '*Guantanamera... Guajira Guantanamera...*' That's it, now the reception is good.

Si vas atrás del mar, atrás del mar,
ahí te sigo.

'Remember that song?'

Of course I remember it. Someone is scrambling about inside the chest. I am rooted to the spot, unable to move, like a roadside cross. Finally, they wrench off the front panels and step outside, shaking off the dust. I cough.

'*Excusez-moi, garçon!*' they say in French.

The figure that steps out has a blond goatee and long, white sideburns. He's wearing a bow tie and a close-fitting tailcoat, with holes under the arms. As he apologizes, he continues to shake off the dust with nervous gestures and then places a monocle in his left eye. His mouth is as wide as old Mick Jagger's.

'*Oh là là!* Let's see now. You're Sam, am I right?'

In Galician, the voice on the radio announces '*Adiós a España*' by Antonio Molina. 'And what's the problem? What does it matter if we enjoy Antonio Molina?' says the presenter.

'Sure we do!' says the other. 'Do you know who Antonio Molina was? Of course you don't. "*Yo quiero ser mataor...*"'

As if surprise has paralyzed my senses as well, it takes me a while to realize what is happening. When he stops talking, the radio can be heard. And vice-versa: when he talks, the sound is lost. That's not the end of the coincidences.

'But...'

'But what, young man?'

'Is that you?'

'No, no! I'm just having a bit of fun. I turn the dial and practise my languages. I've always been very good at languages, ever since I was a child. But what I like best is sacred music. Listen to this. *Tirín, tiririríritirín.*'

'That's amazing!'

'*Tururú, tururururuturú.* Do you think I do it well?'

'That... that's fantastic! It sounds just like an organ.'

'I'm touched, Sam. You have no idea how much an artist likes to be appreciated.'

'Are you a musician?'

'Oh no! Do you want to know who I am?'

Suddenly, his pupils grow much larger while his body shrinks inside his tailcoat and sprouts feathers. He flaps his wings awkwardly and hops up on to the radio.

'Do you really want to know who I am, young man?' says the little owl. 'Do you want to know, young man?'

I am entranced. To be quite honest, I'm not afraid any more. He talks like a circus clown.

'Are you an imp?' I ask out of curiosity. Grandma used

to tell us children that, if you left the saucepan of milk uncovered, you would have to throw it out because the house imp would have washed his bottom in it. 'Are you the house imp?'

'An imp? What's that you're saying? Those are just old wives' tales. I'm something serious. Really serious. Ha, ha!'

Then, for a split second, I see them – the tail and horns.

'The devil! You're the devil!'

I almost shout it out. I'm overjoyed to come across someone so interesting at this time and in the back of beyond. He covers his head with his wings and then slowly peeps out.

'Sh! Keep quiet! Don't be such an ass.'

'Excuse me, I didn't mean to bother you.'

'Besides, you shouldn't be so direct. Use a different name. That's what everybody else does.'

'OK, whatever you decide.'

'Call me "he", for example. Or "sir". Ha, ha! I love being called "sir"!'

'OK, I'll call you "sir".'

'That's it, Sam. You're a good lad. Ha, ha! Right,' he opens wide his beak in a yawn, 'I think I shall retire now, I've worked very hard today.'

'Wait just a moment, sir!'

'What is it, young man?'

'Why do you live here precisely?'

'Because of the garlic! People put out garlic strings to keep me away. They're right, I can't bear garlic, I'm allergic to the stuff, it makes me sick, and there's no garlic in this house. That's all there is to it. There's no garlic here!'

'I mean, why do you live here, in this village? Everybody else is leaving.'

He thinks for a moment. Then he gets in the chest, muttering under his breath, as if he's annoyed.

'Why do you live here? Very good question, young man. You should ask *him*. I'm just an errand boy. That's what I am. An errand boy. Off to sleep! Sweet dreams, my lad!'

The Manor

We are sitting beside the fireplace in the drawing room in Mermaid Manor, in two wobbly armchairs covered in worn fabric. A timid, cold fire is burning, which we lit with the planks of a drawer from the desk. Waves of withered light tremble on Nico's face and interlocked hands.

'What I mean is do you think she was... she was someone special?'

Mermaid Manor must have come into existence like that, like a ruin, with disjointed windows and doors and such large holes in the locks they could hold the hand of a bandit or fugitive. A mansion built for shadows on the loose, so night and cold would have somewhere to hang out during the day. There are lots of pieces of worm-eaten furniture, wood and iron skeletons infected by a sad, sagging epidemic of damp eyes.

'Do you think... it was worth leaving everything because of her?'

Mermaid Manor has the kind of balcony queens appear on when kings are out fighting the Moors. The balustrade is decorated with stone leaves and flowers. Were someone who was not a fair lady, but a man in heavy armour, for example, to lean against it, the whole thing would collapse. On front of the balcony tower is a coat of arms that doesn't show a mermaid, but a palm tree, five birds and a scallop shell.

'She wanted me to leave all this.'

'All what?'

'My job as a policeman.'

On the way back, the wind swirls oak leaves around our feet. We meet Lis, one of the Pancorvos, who is calling to his cattle. Lis, very blond, is about my age. He has an earring and a computer manual under his arm.

'Shit! I thought, if someone really loved you, they loved you because of who you are, not something else, right?'

I picture Sir shaking the dust off his tailcoat, which is torn at the armpits.

'Bah! Who gives a fuck?' says Nico, kicking a gorse bush which still has yellow flowers.

'*Eivacave, somorenavai!*'

It sounds like old Pancorvo's voice coming from a loudspeaker in the valley, but it's Lis, the one with the earring, calling to his cattle.

The Illness

Old Brandariz comes around and knocks at the door. Grandma Herminia is watching at the window, and I think she's happy it's him and they've finally broken their silence. But the man is all worked up, and his lips tremble when he speaks.

'The girl. The girl's in a bad way. Really bad.'

'Poor thing!'

Nico rushes to get the car out of the shed. Gaby brings the baby out of the house in a Moses basket, and I open the back door. When the car pulls away, she looks at us with unease, and I am reminded of an actress outside the cinema, wanting to run away from everybody, in dark glasses.

'It won't be a problem,' says grandma, and she invites us in for a coffee.

At the kitchen table, as they discuss old and young people's ailments, I feel rage welling up inside me. I rise to my feet and bound up the stairs.

'Where are you going, boy?' asks grandma.

'I'll be back in a minute.'

I lift the trapdoor and jump into the attic. I switch on the light and bang on the chest a couple of times.

'Hey, you, sir!'

Nothing. Not a peep. I pull back one of the planks and see it's empty.

'Sir, sir! If you can hear me, please say something.'

I notice the radio. 'I turn the dial and practise my languages.' I plug it in and rotate the knob. Country music. An explosion in Belfast. Snow above 800 metres. The Pope in Africa. The Pope in Africa! Just a minute. Music by Bach.

'Hey, sir, listen! I know you're in there.'

His appearance this time is really rather extraordinary. He is wearing a leopard skin over his shoulders, tight, black leather trousers and a belt with a large, silver buckle. His skin is all dark, his eyebrows plucked, his lips fleshy. He's trying to imitate Prince or something.

'Listen, young man. I'm very busy. You can't just get me to come out whenever you feel like it.'

'No, you listen, sir. If something happens to the girl, I'll kill you. In God's name, I'll kill you.'

He looks surprised, as if I've parted from the script. He must be feeling awkward in all this get-up, or perhaps it's the cold. The truth is he shakes himself and turns pale and elegant. Hello, old Bowie.

'I think there's been a terrible mistake. Who do you think I am? I don't go about killing children.'

'They've taken the little girl to the hospital!'

'It's nothing serious. Nutritional problems. The mother's milk is a little sad. Too sad. She'll get by.'

'Swear it to me!'

'I can't swear, but I give you my word.'

'OK then. I believe you.'

'Thank you, Sam. Thank you for believing in me. I'm going back now, I left mid-ceremony. *Addio!*'

When I go downstairs, grandma is on her own, peeling potatoes.

'May I know what the hell you're up to! No, don't laugh.'

'Nothing will happen to the baby, grandma. You can be sure of that. Nothing will happen to her.'

The Glow-Worm

Nico arrives in the early morning. I'm in bed, pretending to be asleep, and wait until he has undressed. He places the revolver under his pillow.

'What happened?'

'The girl is weak, but they say she'll be OK.'

'And Gaby?'

'She stayed with the child. In maternity.'

'That's where I was born.'

'What do you mean? You were born in a taxi, which had a flat tyre.'

'I know! I don't see why you have to adopt such an obnoxious tone.'

'I didn't adopt an obnoxious tone.'

'Oh, go to hell!'

Nico doesn't snore. He stays awake all night. I also don't sleep, but that's just the way I am. I see him get out of bed and pace up and down in the half-light. He rummages in the pockets of my clothes and lights a cigarette. I'm about to speak, to tell him off or something, but make up my mind to leave him alone. He sits on the bed with his head bowed. The cigarette resembles a solitary glow-worm.

'You don't look too well, my boy,' says grandma, serving us some milk. Nico has huge bags under his eyes. Bigger than mine. And darker. Mine are violet.

'Why don't you go back to bed?'

'It's nothing, grandma,' says Nico. 'I'll get some sleep soon enough.'

'Do you want me to wash the car? I can wash it if you like,' I ask him.

'You, wash the car?'

'That's right. Me. Why shouldn't I? It wouldn't be the first time.'

'It would. The first time you've done something useful.'

'Let him wash it,' says grandma.

'Do as you please! Just make sure you don't scratch it!'

'I won't wash it then. You and the car can rot in hell!'

It's drizzling in the yard. I know this rain, tricky and false, it slips inside your head and turns you into a vegetable. All things considered, it would be a bit dumb to wash the car. It's enough to take it out of the shed and let this relentless lady do the job instead.

In the shed, next to the car, is the family cart, its shaft propped on the ground. There aren't any oxen to pull it. But it's still there, whole, solid, seemingly prepared to go singing down the tracks of Aita at any minute. Unlike other old things, which are cornered and fearful, there's something strange about this cart. It's like a tool. It seems to be waiting, calm, unconcerned about its future destiny, like an animal that watches hail through the window of its stall. Both strong and childish – that's what the toys of giants must have been: the models of spaceships belonging to alien potato eaters. It's as if, not so long ago, superior beings inhabited these parts who were capable of shaping wood and stone.

How on earth did grandpa set about making a cart? The bowl of wine was like a thimble in his hands. From time to time, he would play the clarinet, which he kept in a green cloth on top of the wardrobe. The keys were like buttons in his cracked fingers, which bore traces of earth right down to the bottom of his nails.

At the back of the shed is his carpenter's workbench. The ground below is still strewn with wood shavings. On the wall, hanging in geometrical order, the handsaws, brushes, adze, hammer, mallet, brace and box of nails. I grab a stick and drive three nails into one end, like a star. That's all I know how to do.

'What are you up to, Samuel? Take care with those nails!'

'You know something, grandma? I'm going to build a cart.'

'Where are you going?'

'I'll be back soon.'

'I'm coming too.'

He doesn't want to let me. I take up position in the middle of the yard and cross my arms. I think it's possible he might have run me down, had grandma's silhouette not appeared in the doorway. I decide to adopt a relaxed attitude.

'You're a bastard, a selfish bastard. It's not enough for you to embitter our lives. You want us to run around after you all day.'

'You brought me here. It wasn't me. You're the one who brought me here.'

'Oh, shut the fuck up!'

He puts a tape in the cassette player. Rap. How strange. It's the story of a guy who wants to enter a disco, but the bouncer doesn't let him. They must have started selling this kind of stuff in petrol stations as well. We travel along the road to the West and then divert on to forest tracks. Pine trees line the hillsides, clinging to the shirt tails of cliffs that have broad cheeks and a forehead like Frankenstein's. The car starts to descend, shaking its snout. On the right is Mount Branco with its glistening skirt of shells. Down below – wheeee! – is Trece Beach. A special-effects film. If you give the sea a dragon's mouth and a winged horse's neigh, you can imagine something similar. The ideal place to be shipwrecked once and for all.

'Are we going down there?'

'I am.'

I'm sure those tracks in the sand belong to a wolf or something worse. Nico walks in front, seemingly hypnotized by that raging sea with its desire to gobble down lunar cycles and the barrier of mountains. I'm afraid he might carry on, enter the foam and leave me alone. But no, he walks parallel to me. Footprints are better defined in wet sand. The neigh is ear-piercing and keeps you company.

'Nicooo!'

He's twenty yards away, with his back to me and his hands in his pockets.

'You're right, Nico! I'm a bastard!'

The neigh sends back my words. I can almost see them, as clearly drawn as my footprints.

'I'm a walking disaster!'

It's funny. I feel well. I have the impression I'm talking sense at last.

'I'm a selfish, gibbering wreck!'

Nico sits on a rock, closes his eyes and leans back with his mouth open.

'I'm a twat!'

Well, I'm not sure about that. Not a twat exactly. I'm closer to him now. I don't know whether to say it. I hope he doesn't hear me this time either.

'Go back to Rosa, Nico! Go back to her!'

It's not easy breathing in this watery wind. I lick my lips. It's a nice taste. Nico is over there. He opens his eyes and turns his head.

'You look like a madman. What on earth were you shouting?'

'Oh, nothing. A pile of nonsense.'

The Prison

Nico sits all evening at the kitchen table. He doesn't seem to be reading the magazine because the pages are upside down, two glasses of Martini with ice and a slice of lemon hooked over the edge on the verge of spilling on the tablecloth, which is made of tulle with blue crowns, birds and floral designs. He's in a mood. If you don't move, that drizzle gets inside your head, dampens your spirit. You should never stop when you're in prison, Luou told me once, whatever you do, don't stop.

I'm doing exercises in the kitchen. One, arms back; two, arms up, trying to touch the beam where the ham is suspended; three, arms down to the tip – uff! – of my toes.

Grandma is sweeping the floor. I grab the broom and finish for her. Then I hold the broom like a bass guitar and play a tune worthy of the band Anthrax.

'You were just like that as a child,' cackles grandma. 'Always playing around! You never stopped.'

Nico carries on hiding under his arms.

The Photographs

Grandma keeps the photographs in a Segarra Shoes cardboard box. There's one with the whole family, my mother as a girl wearing a white diadem. Everyone's there – my grandparents, my mother's sisters, Uncle Lito with his bike and trousers tucked into his socks. They're all in their Sunday best. Grandpa has a tie, and you can see the imprint of his beret on his flattened hair. They're out in the yard. On the left, the well with the pulley and zinc bucket. The door, open as always, and, leaning against the jamb, a smiling young man.

'Who's that?'

'A day labourer,' says grandma, also surprised. 'A Portuguese man we hired.'

He has a scarf around his neck. He reminds me of... what was his name?... that's it, James Dean.

'What are you laughing at?'

'Oh, nothing.'

'A Portuguese man. He turned up one day without anything, just his hands in his pockets, and asked for work, something with which to pay for his food and a shed to sleep in. Your grandpa said, "This boy is running away from somebody." I said, "Don't be daft, he looks like a good enough person." I remember he sang some very beautiful songs. He was always the way he is in the photo, always smiling. One day, he said he had to leave. I asked him why, and he said, "Because of you, my lady." And then he kissed my hand.' Grandma smiles like a little girl. 'The things that happen in life!'

'What about grandpa?'

'I never told him about it. He said, "I told you he was running away from somebody."'

There is also a photo of me at my First Communion.

The Fire

When the kitchen light is switched off, the threads of bodies relax, and eyes are drawn to the fire as if by magic. The flames from the smaller sticks clamber up the bark of the log, kissing it with their serpent tongues, enveloping it in a triumphant, devouring embrace. Each piece of wood is consumed by a slightly different fire. Yellow has a red heart and blue wings with white spots. What colour do bodies give off when they burn? Those that are incinerated, reduced to a handful of ashes, how much red, yellow, blue, white lace, do they produce? I've heard it said human bodies smell awful when cremated, like a worn tyre braking on tarmac. The pages of the magazine also smell bad. But the colours are vibrant. I can see Caroline going up in green and lilac, the ice of the Martinis melting in a white that is almost black. And there I go, in my First Communion outfit, dressed as a sailor, not wanting to burn, curling up like a hedgehog, turning into a sheet of ash without flames or anything.

The Cot

The relentless lady bangs on the roof and windows. I smoke, leaning against the bedhead, blowing rings in order to ignore her. Nico is awake as well.

'Nico, do you fancy a cigarette?'

'Me? No. Why should I?'

'Oh, I was just wondering.'

He stares at the wall. I think he's staring at my sailing boat in the storm.

'In 1970, you weren't born yet.'

'What was it like when I was born?'

'Mother would knit and sew all day long. She would say, "You're going to have a little brother." When you arrived from hospital, there were lots of people in the house. Mother's sisters came, women from next door. I remember them saying, "Look, look, here's your little brother." But I ran away and hid in the cupboard.'

'Ha.'

'Then, when everybody was in the sitting room, talking and drinking coffee, I went slowly to our parents' bedroom. You were in the cot, wrapped in a woollen blanket. All I could see were your eyes and tiny little hands. I spoke to you, whispered things to you. I thought... I thought you might be able to reply. And I would defend you always.'

'Ha.'

'Samuel.'

'What?'

'Have you taken Something? I mean, have you been taking Something on the quiet?'

'No way, man! I promise you I haven't. Why?'

'Oh, nothing.'

I take another drag. The lady's eyes now silently slide down the window.

'You know? I think I might go up to the attic.'

'To the attic? You're off your head. What are you going to do in the attic?'

'There's a radio, remember? That old radio that used to be in the kitchen. I think I might be able to fix it. The other night, when you took Gaby's child to hospital, I was fiddling around with it and could hear something. I think the valves are a bit loose.'

'Don't wake grandma.'

'I won't.'

The Bastard

The chest panels have been completely ripped off, and the interior is empty. There's something strange in the air. I place my hands on the radio, and it seems to me that the wood shines as good as new, without dust. The other objects, the framework of the attic, have the same gleam. There are no cobwebs on the beams or tiles, and the light of the bulb is more intense.

'Hey, sir! Where are you?'

I switch on the radio and turn the dial. I can't hear anything very well. Just a background hum, like that of an angry swarm.

'Hey, sir! I want to talk to you!'

I bang on the radio. The hum goes and comes back.

'Where on earth are you? There's something important I want to talk about.'

Suddenly, the music becomes very clear. It's a funeral march. I rotate the dial, slowly to begin with, then frenetically. I go from MW to SW to LW. On every station, every wave, the same music, a solemn, painful organ, an organ that pierces my senses and judders along my veins.

'Where are you, you bastard? Where are you?'

I unplug the radio, but it's no use. The march carries on relentlessly. I prick up my ears. I'm quite sure I heard a guffaw in all the music. Followed by footsteps on the roof.

'Sir, sir! Are you up there?'

I feverishly remove some tiles until I've made a hole which allows me to stick my head out into the night. There he is, playing with the moonlight in the pupils of his eyes, which grow and shrink to the rhythm of his guffaws. His feathers are ruffled by the breeze, like a cassock.

'Listen, don't be such a bastard. I know you're Help. I know that now.'

The little owl stops playing with its eyes and stares at me. It then flies off in the direction of the bell tower. From the attic, the prayers of a sinister choir ascend towards the stars.

'Help, don't do this to me! Come back, Help, come back!'

The little bastard laughs. I'm quite sure he's laughing.

Today, lament. Do you know what that is, Sam? To really weep. Something you can't do. When the tears well up in your eyes, pour down your cheeks and enter your nose, and you drink them, with their salty taste.

'You're a bastard, a real son of a bitch! I'll kill you! You hear me? I'll kill you!'

The lights go on in some of Aita's windows. I return to the radio and hurl it on the floor.

'Bastard, you're a bastard!'

My whole body is trembling, and I'm very, very cold.

'Samuel! What is it, Samuel?'

Nico grabs my shoulders and gives me a shake. His eye sockets appear empty.

'Samuel! Listen to me, Samuel!'

'You're a bastard, a son of a bitch!'

'It's me, Sam, your brother.'

'Bastard, bastard, bastard!'

'Shut up, Sam, or I'll wallop you!'

Nico throws me on the sacks and takes off his belt.

'What a bastard, what a bastard! Shoot him, Nico! He's up in the bell tower, Nico, in the bell tower!'

'God damn it, Sam, what have you been taking? Tell me, what have you been taking?'

'Leave him, leave him to me,' says grandma. 'Poor little boy!'

'Shoot him, Nico, shoot him!'

Grandma fetches a blanket and wraps it around me. It's one of those blankets where the apples sleep. She sits beside me and places my head in her lap. I'm sweating and cold. She carries on stroking me until I gradually fall into the black warmth of her tummy.

'Don't let him get away...'

The Eve of March

I wake up in grandma's bed. She's sleeping in that way she has, stretched out, facing upwards, her skin white as flour, her hands interlocked on her chest as if she's praying. The lady with her mantle of tears has gone, and light filters through all the cracks in the house in Aita. That is when I hear Princess howling in the granary. It's an unending, pitiable whine.

'Grandma, grandma, I feel OK. Grandma, can you hear me? Hey, grandma, see what a beautiful day! Grandma, grandma. Come on, wake up, grandma! Why don't you wake up?'

'How's that leg?' asks the hospital porter.

'Take a look at this!' I jump like a Comanche in the direction of the lift. It's amazing! Everybody seems to know me, and in Orthopaedics they almost clap their hands, smiling radiantly.

'Hello, Sam!'

'Hello, darling!'

I'm on the verge of throwing myself into Miss Cowbutt's arms, and for that to be the end of the story.

'I'm off to see Luou! Is he still dressed up as a Martian?'

'Wait, wait, just a moment,' she says with a half-smile. 'I have to tell you something.'

'What is it, gorgeous?'

'It's no joke,' she says, wiping the smile off her face. 'It has to do with your friend.'

'...'

'Your friend won't walk again.'

'What do you mean?'

'He's not going to walk again.'

I gaze down the corridor. There's a woman in a pink dressing gown.

'Tell me something.'

'Yes?'

'Will he be able to drive? Travel in a car or something?'

'...'

'I know there are some people who do this. I once saw

a man in a wheelchair. They put him in a car, and he drove. That's true, isn't it?'

The Outlaws

'Thanks for the call, Sam. I knew I could trust you.'

Don is more squidgy than ever, like an overgrown raisin. Perhaps, when they opened him up in hospital, some more air went in. He's propped up on his cushions, in a large wicker armchair, with Tip and Top, smiling, to his left and right.

'So you've been in the country. I like the country a lot, Sam. Everything's so green, so pure!'

'I don't like it.'

'Ah, right, not that kind of country. I'm talking about real countryside, one without gorse, manure, mud or people with grim looks, always dressed in black.'

'And crows everywhere,' I add. 'Crows are like tramps, like outlaws.'

'Ha, ha, like outlaws!' says Tip.

'Yeah, ha, ha, like outlaws!' says Top.

'What I like,' says Don, 'is countryside that's been properly looked after. A nice house with a large lawn and trees in flower, camellias, rhododendrons, things like that. Nicely positioned trees like bonsais. A pretty house with a porch to sit on and take the air as the sun goes down and the finches sing. You know, Sam? I'm thinking of building a house like that. I'll invite everybody, all my friends, to play golf and have a drink as the sun goes down.'

'That would be great, Don.'

'You'll see, Sam. It'll be a pretty house, a wonderful house. A house in which to live at ease and grow old, because the years go by, Sam, the years go by.'

'Yeah, ha, ha, grow old!' says Tip.

'What are you talking about, Don! Grow old!' says Top.

'You know, Don? While I was in Aita, my grandmother died.'

'Oh, I'm sorry to hear that, Sam! Really sorry.'

'She was very, very old. Actually, I'm not even sure how old she was.'

'Yes, of course. What are you doing, standing there like a couple of chatterboxes? Give my friend here Something. Something Real.'

The Month of the Potatoes

My mother crosses the yard. She doesn't look down, but I follow in her footsteps. Wherever she steps, there is no water. Behind us is the door of Aita, which has been double-locked. I have the key in my hand. A cold, slightly rusty key. The taxi passes in front of the cemetery, and my mother crosses herself, 'by the sign of the Holy Cross'. Like silhouettes behind the glass of an aquarium, I see Dombodán and the Blue Child with his little guitar, sitting on a gravestone. The car overtakes

Lucas' cart, which is surrounded by the warm mist rising off a load of manure. Piles of the stuff, put there to feed the earth, smoke in the fields, under the rain.

'Oh, goodness me, where did I put the key?'

'I have it, mother.'

'Take good care of it.'

'Yes, mother.'

'Take good care of it. Whatever you do, don't lose it.'

The car suddenly accelerates, clears a way through the silvery curtain. By the roadside, shadows, stooping under burdens of green and mist, head in the other direction and pass through the gold ring of mimosas.

Read more Galician fiction in English from Small Stations Press:

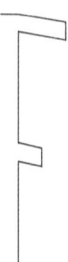

Manuel Rivas, ONE MILLION COWS

From the author of *The Low Voices* and *The Carpenter's Pencil*, the book of short stories that set him on his way and revolutionized Galician literature when it came out at the end of the 1980s. For the first time, Galician prose dealt with the Galician landscape in a modern context, uniting tradition and modernity, placing the poetry of landscape alongside the irony of modern society. In *One Million Cows*, a collection of eighteen short stories by Manuel Rivas, the first he published, a boy tries to find out if his cousin is really a battery-operated robot, a sailor who has been shipwrecked at sea turns up dead in a local bar, the inhabitants of a village transport a young suicide so that he can be buried in an adjoining parish, a Galician who has recently returned from England dreams of building a golf course on the mud-flats of his childhood, and a prospective councillor is put off by the fish scales on a fishwife's hands. Manuel Rivas is Galicia's most international author, and once again the reader will be able to enjoy his striking metaphors, his commitment to what he writes, and his lingering eye for detail.

ISBN 978-954-384-035-9

Miguel-Anxo Murado, ASH WEDNESDAY

In this collection of sixteen short stories by the Galician writer Miguel-Anxo Murado, the reader is taken on a journey through the various rites of passage that make up an individual's life, from the months-old baby who lives in the eternal moment of Nothingness and quickly forgets an argument with his elder brother to the university professor who visits a colleague in Kyoto to see the cherry blossom and before the symbols of impermanence is forced to confront his own terminal illness. Children and adults alike endure extreme situations, from a child who is bullied at school to the Chinese women workers who stay up all night to prepare a handmade suit for the morning. Sailors are rescued at sea; others are cast adrift when their ship sinks, at the mercy of the current. A young man is brought face to face with his late father when surrounded by a mountain blaze; a young girl endeavors to learn the secrets to her sister's radiant beauty. Two boys fall for the same girl; one tries to curry favor with the members of his gang in a story reminiscent of Isaac Babel's *Red Cavalry*, while another searches for the strength inside. All are caught in unexpected situations, elegantly and expertly described, and handed the task of how to react in a book that celebrates the human spirit across barriers of time and language.

ISBN 978-954-384-053-3

Miguel Anxo Fernández, A NICHE FOR MARILYN

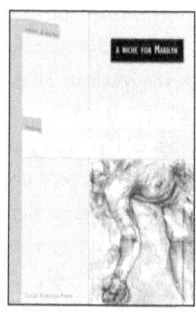

Frank Soutelo is a down-at-heel private detective, the son of Galician immigrants, based in Los Angeles, California. He doesn't get much choice in his assignments and has to take pretty much what's on offer, so when he gets hired and paid an advance of twenty-five thousand dollars, he's understandably pleased, and his secretary even more so. The unusual thing, however, is what he's been asked to do: to recover the body of the actress Marilyn Monroe, which has reputedly gone missing from her grave in Westwood Village Memorial Park Cemetery. Big Frank, as he is known, is about to get drawn into a world that is unfamiliar to him: a world of necrophiliacs, zealous watchmen, uniformed chauffeurs and high-class mansions. The question is will he be able to extricate himself from this situation with his dignity and heart in one piece?

ISBN 978-954-384-051-9

Xurxo Borrazás, VICIOUS

Shakespearean drama set in a Galician context. There is something strikingly postmodern – or Elizabethan – about this novel, in which a man from Laracha, south-west of Coruña, on Galicia's famed Coast of Death, is on the run for committing a multiple murder that shocks the local community and has the priest calling for the razing of the local slums. Chucho Monteiro, who has always been overlooked by his father in favor of his younger brother, Daniel, more pliable, less violent, heads to the port of Coruña in order to effect his escape on the first ship weighing anchor, a ship that will take him not to Stratford, but to Southampton and on. In a fascinating, multi-layered narrative, the author keeps the reader guessing about the murderer's final destination until the very end. Narrative chronology is mixed up, and the veil between author and reader is torn in two, so that we're not sure if we are witnesses or partakers of this narrative. *Vicious* (called *Criminal* in Galician) is Xurxo Borrazás' second and best-known novel, and won him the Spanish Critics' Prize as well as the San Clemente Prize awarded by high-school readers.

ISBN 978-954-384-038-0

Suso de Toro, POLAROID

One of the most exciting works of literature to have come out of Galicia in the last thirty years, and the first adult-fiction title by Suso de Toro to be made available in the English-language market. There is something startling about this book. With Raymond Carver-like simplicity, the author extracts the commonplace events and ordinary frustrations of life, shedding light on them, exalting them and undermining them at the same time, so that the reader is left in a hiatus, expectant and fulfilled. What goes on here is impossible, outrageous, and yet it happens. A blind man beats and is poisoned by his wife, an aged housemaid tries to breastfeed the baby when the parents are out, a second-hand typewriter insists on typing out its own message, a rapist awaits the family's vengeance while wishing he knew the victim's name, a cash machine flirts with a customer of the bank by making spurious deposits into her account, a jumper turns murderous, a porn model seeks an intimate relationship that isn't confined to the glossy pages of a magazine, a mother loses track of her child, Cain and Abel appear in modern dress, the hero Theseus is driven to question whether he really is a hero or not, a man finds his wife having an affair in the wardrobe... There is something absolutely surprising about these stories that signalled a new direction in post-Franco Galician literature, in a book the author himself described as 'an outburst of fury inspired by punk.'

ISBN 978-954-384-036-6

For an up-to-date list of our publications, please visit
www.smallstations.com

For more information on Galician literature in English, please visit
www.galicianliterature.gal